I DON'T KNOW I SAID

I Don't Know

a novel by Matthew Savoca

I Said

Publishing Genius Press
Baltimore 2013

Publishing Genius Press
Baltimore, Maryland

www.publishinggenius.com
IDKIS.tumblr.com
www.matthewsavoca.com

ISBN 13: 978-0-9887503-1-9
First published in April 2013

For my dog Sabre
1978 – 1993

ONE

The United States

Neither of us had jobs or hobbies. We didn't have anywhere to be or anything to be doing. It had been that way for a while. It was August now. It was hot. We'd left town a few weeks before, planning to be gone for a long time. Whenever someone asked how long we'd be gone Carolina would say a year or more. But we'd returned already and in the meantime Carolina's parents had cleaned and straightened up the apartment in preparation to sublet it. They did a really good job too because when we got back it didn't feel like getting back to anywhere. It didn't feel like going home. It was another new place. We'd been to a lot of them—everything foreign, everything indifferent. The apartment didn't care. The front door, the toilet, the blinds on the windows, they didn't seem like ours anymore and that felt nice in a way to me.

I think it upset Carolina a bit. She wanted the city to care. She wanted the world to care. She wanted us to care—me to care. She always accused me of being sleepy. One day I was watching something on the Internet and I guess I was laughing pretty hard because Carolina was surprised. She came into the living room from the kitchen and said, "You never laugh like that." I shrugged my shoulders. She went back into the kitchen and after a few minutes I went in there and sat at one of the high chairs. "Hearing you laugh like that made me realize how sleepy you are most of the time. You are barely alive," she said.

I didn't know what to say. "I'm not sleepy," I said. "Don't call me sleepy."

I had been the first one through the door after I turned the key hard and got it open. The deadbolt didn't remember me. "Where did everything go?" I said walking down the hallway.

"What everything?" Carolina said.

"The stuff," I said. "All the stuff we left."

"It's all here somewhere." She said they said they just put everything away neatly.

"But where?" I said.

We stood at different ends of the hallway. Carolina had this look on her face. It was like we had accidentally walked into someone else's apartment and she felt embarrassed. We didn't talk about it, we only stared at each other and then discussed eating lunch. We agreed we would. Then we ate. Afterward we sat in the living room. It was almost empty. We were Indian-style on the floor. We talked about the future without knowing what we were talking about. I said, "I don't know," and stared at the floor. Carolina said, "Me neither." I said, "I'll do whatever," and she said, "So will I." We didn't know what to do, so we went for a walk. We moved our legs for a long time in one direction and then turned around. At some point I said, "I feel a strong desire to choose a thing and call it bullshit."

"Pick me," she said.

When we got home I stared at the ceiling fan and made a noise that sounded like "haaauuuuugh," but more nasal and droning. Usually Carolina was the one to exorcise things vocally in strange sounds or silly little songs. I was more for eye movements. Sometimes I'd move my eyes in a lot of little directions very rapidly—diagonal lines, circular motions, random sequences—just because.

I was lying diagonally on the bed. Carolina was doing yoga on the floor at the foot of the bed. Her yoga mat was blue, I could see the color reflected in one of the fan blades above me. She said, "Yoga makes me feel like everything is okay, like I'm okay, and you're okay, and." She stopped talking as if it were natural to end with the word "and."

"And what?" I said flatly. I remember not caring at all, about anything. My head was turned, my cheek flat on the mattress. I was looking at Carolina with one eye, the other blocked off by the bunched-up duvet, probably crossing itself, saying Hail Marys. She was in Virasana. Her shins were flat on the ground from foot to knee, knees bent fully with her behind resting on her ankles; her torso extended out and down at a slight angle with her arms stretched out like superman, palms on the floor. She didn't answer my question. I looked at the ceiling and then down out the top of the window at a bird going by.

Later we were reading together on the couch with our legs interlocked and she said, "I'd feel better if we chose a thing and then did it."

"Okay," I said.

We went to see Carolina's grandmother the next day. She had recently become pretty sick and mostly stayed in bed. Maybe that was why we'd come home, or maybe we just told ourselves that was why. Any reason to go somewhere or do something, any reason at all, and we'd do it.

At her house, I washed the dishes in a cast iron sink that was divided into two equally sized parts. I let the water run. The ceiling fan was on but not the light, so I turned it on. I put all the glasses on the bottom shelf of the drying rack, and the plates and bowls on top. I washed the silverware and put it in a metal cylinder with holes to let the water drain out. I filled the pots with water and put some dish soap inside and let them sit while I left the kitchen to go back to the bedroom. Carolina was there with her grandmother. She had cancer in her lungs.

"So when are you leaving?" her grandmother asked.

"We don't know yet. Maybe this week." Carolina said.

"Thought you were supposed to leave already."

"We did. We left and then we came back. We're back now."

"Oh," she said, "you didn't come back for me, did you?" Then right away she said, "This woman thinks that arugula is the cure for people who are dying. She makes me eat it at every meal. I can't stand her."

She was talking about the live-in caretaker, an elderly Romanian woman who kept a copy of the Bible and an orthodox crucifix by her bed in the spare bedroom. Later when we left and were walking home Carolina had said, "My grandmother does not like her at all. It's a problem."

"It's harder at the beginning," I'd said. "It will get better when they get used to each other."

"My grandmother is not very easy," she'd said, "I just hope she doesn't try to talk to her about God or whatever. That will be it for her."

I hadn't said anything to that.

When I first entered the bedroom, her grandmother asked me if I wanted any ice cream or iced tea or anything at all to drink or eat. "No, thank you," I said. She asked me again five minutes later and I said, "Okay," and then went and poured myself iced tea and I drank it. It was pleasant to drink. I went back to the bedroom with the empty glass in my hand so she would see it.

"Carolee, get him some iced tea, would you?" she said.

"No, no, got it myself. I drank it already," I said. "It was good."

"Have more, more," she said and made a motion with her arm. It took so long for it to get up into the air and then back down to rest.

"I'm okay for now, thank you," I said.

"Are you sure?" she said, "Because Steven bought it, he'll buy more, there's plenty more."

"I'm okay now, thanks," I said. It could have gone on like that for longer but Carolina said that we had to get going.

"We have to go now. We're having lunch with mom's parents."

"Oh, you're not having lunch here?" her grandmother said.

"No, they just got back and it was Grampa's birthday yesterday."

"Oh, say happy birthday for me."

"Okay, I will."

"And come back and see me before you leave again."

"Okay, yes. Bye Grandma."

"Bye, thank you for the visit."

"Bye, bye."

"Bye."

"Bye."

"Bye."

And there was waving. Hands were the last things to be seen.

It was a long walk. When we got home we were sweating. It was hot out, so we each took our pants off and sat on the couch. Carolina tossed her jeans on the floor and I folded mine, placed them neatly on a chair and thought about how that was something I cared about—clothes placed neatly. I went into the kitchen and poured water into a glass and drank some. Then I gave the rest to Carolina. We washed ourselves and then caught the bus to go to lunch. We waited a long time for the bus and Carolina was hot and sweating, much more than me. I tried to get her to stand in the shade of the bus schedule sign but she would only do it for a few seconds, then walk away. I watched a bird, the sky, and a middle-aged Korean woman kicking a rock up the sidewalk. When the bus finally came it was so cold inside that the sweat on Carolina's neck froze and gave her cramps which she felt at night when we were trying to sleep.

We had lunch with grandparents two and three. The usual lunch: a lot of food, too much cheese. Ancient pictures. Stories to go along with them. An anecdote about Abraham Lincoln, how some little girl from Kansas had convinced him to grow a beard so that people would take him more seriously.

When we left their apartment, we left with a lot of dried garlic cloves and fresh hot peppers. At home again we planned to rest and not do anything except watch reruns of *Sex and the City* or something else, anything easy so that we didn't have to think about whatever, but we ended up going out to see a friend of Carolina's downtown. Neither of us wanted to go, but we both kind of wanted to go, and for some reason thought we should go, so we went. The bus was late and had trouble getting past the arena because there was a Madonna concert. "I hate being late, this is awful," Carolina said.

"It's okay," I said.

"It's not okay, we aren't going to be a little late, we are going to be half an hour late."

I sent a text message that said, "We are going to be a little late," and got a message back that said, "It's okay, I'll go for a walk and meet you at the fountain at 8." I told Carolina but she just stared at the floor of the bus. I looked at her and then out the window.

After a few minutes she said, "This is ridiculous."

"What is?" I said.

"We are."

"Why do you have to be so negative?" I said. "It's fine, whatever. It doesn't matter. You'll feel better."

"I don't want to even go now. I didn't want to go before."

"It will be nice to walk around at night, in the air."

"But what are we going to do? We didn't even think of something to do."

"It doesn't matter, we will just do whatever. Something will happen and it will be okay."

"I feel better when I'm by myself. I get nervous when you're with me," she said.

"What? Why?"

"I don't know, I just do."

I didn't say anything. She didn't say anything either and soon the bus arrived at our stop and we got off and laughed about some guy's small, tight shorts as we waited for the light to turn green so we could walk across the street.

We walked through the park and then went towards Center City. We walked around for a few hours, stopping to get ice cream and sit down for a while. At eleven, Carolina and I took the bus home. It was normally a thirty-minute trip but it took almost two hours because now the Madonna concert was over and people were everywhere, not letting the buses pass for long stretches of time. We talked about getting off and walking home as if we knew it were the better thing to do, but we just stayed on the bus, not moving or talking or doing anything at all.

At home we drank water, brushed our teeth, and went to bed. In bed Carolina felt the pain in her neck. "It's that stupid bus's fault," she said.

"Do you want me to turn the fan off?" I said.

"No, it's okay," she said, "you need it."

In the spring the year before, right around the time Carolina would have been graduating if she had been able to write her thesis, she got into a pretty bad car accident. She was in intensive care for a short while, but then they took her out of there to a regular room where I could see her. About a week after that they transferred her to a hospital in Maryland, and I stayed away because they said it would be better if she didn't have visitors for a while. I went to my parents' instead of staying at our place because it was easier to avoid thinking too much about anything, and there was always something going on to keep me a little busy. My brother had moved back in after getting engaged, wanting to save money, so his fiancée was always around, and my parents were around. It just seemed easier, and it was, but during the last few days it was harder, and the last night especially, so I decided to go see a movie. I left the house earlier than I had planned and waited a long time in the parking lot for the theater to open. They didn't unlock the doors until a few minutes before the show—the first

show of the day—around five o'clock. It was a small non-
profit theater owned by the township, with just two small
working screens and one big one that was waiting on more
funding to have the remodeling finished. I was alone in the
theater, which was nice because it meant I could change
seats as many times as I wanted without feeling like I was
disturbing anyone. I didn't, though. I picked one seat and
stayed in it until the lights came on, past the credits, and
even longer. The cleaning person, who was the same person
as the ticket selling person and the ticket checking person
and the little snack counter person, came in the side door
with a broom and a dustpan—one of those ones on a pole
so you don't have to bend over. I watched her walk around
the theater looking for trash. She moved like a hand truck.
There was nothing to clean because I had been the only one
in there and I hadn't put any trash on the ground, so she left.

Then I got up and left the theater. I walked through
the long lobby out the glass doors to the street, which was
empty. There were streetlamps on and I looked up as I
walked under them to my dad's car and then drove it to
his home which was not far away. The night was cool and
pleasant so I drove around for a while. At home, I ate a bowl
of cut up fruit that I found in the refrigerator. There was a
note on it that said "I left you most of the strawberries—
Mom." There was a little heart drawn in ink at the bottom.
It was late and the house was dark. I sat at the kitchen table
and looked out into the backyard that I couldn't really see.
I knew there was a creek and some trees and a log. I walked
into the room with the computer in it and jiggled the mouse
but the screen stayed dark so I lay down on a couch and then

moved to the floor. I thought about how I had not made a noise with my mouth in a lot of hours. I tried to count how many hours and I counted eleven but then I remembered that I spoke when I bought the movie ticket, so it was only really three hours which I decided was not a lot of hours. Then I thought that my mouth had probably made some noises while I was eating and so it was really only about twenty minutes.

In the morning I left early and walked to the train station and got on a bus. I stayed on the bus until it got to a big bus station and then I changed buses. I chose a seat on the new bus, which was a long distance bus, and then changed my mind two or three times before sitting down. Then I changed my decision and went to a different seat. The bus started moving and I was alone on it and I thought about being the only person on the bus and in the world. I wondered how long the trip would be and whether or not I had chosen the best seat. "Maybe there is a better seat somewhere," I was thinking. I sat up and looked around the bus. The driver looked at me in the mirror with his eyes and I saw his eyes with mine. I could see on his face that he was going to speak and then he did. "Got this whole bus to yourself," he said. I smiled instead of saying something.

"Lucky thing, too, they need it at the depot or we wouldn't be running. Usually don't make the trip for less than a quarter load but it's just as well for me. I'm goin' home," he said.

"What do they do with the people if there's less than a quarter load?" I said.

"What's that?"

"The passengers, what happens to the ones there are if there's less than a quarter load?"

"Well I guess if they cancel the trip, they refund their money, but I wouldn't right know it, I'm just the wheel-and-pedals man," he said.

I nodded and sat further down and put my back against the seat. I looked out the window and saw people driving cars. I saw some of their faces. I closed my eyes and listened to the sound of the bus on the road. It felt calm and good to be moving—good to be alone and moving.

When we got to the station, I asked the driver how to get to the hospital. He didn't know the place I was asking about so I told him a street name. "Just walk east on that road we're starin' at. If you get wet, you went too far," he said. He had a southern accent that I didn't notice the first time he spoke. His words were long and slow. I thought of the Mason-Dixon line, then said thanks and got down off the bus, crossing over in front, putting on my backpack and clasping the strap across my chest. I didn't know if I was going the right way. I turned back towards the bus driver who was already looking at me. He pointed in the other direction and said something. I didn't hear what he said, but I knew he meant I had to go the other way. I waved at him and walked in the direction he pointed. I said thanks as I went by. He was reading a newspaper. He just put his hand up in the air, held it there for a second, and then brought it back down to the wheel. As I passed houses, I wondered where the bus driver lived and why he wasn't off the bus and going home.

I called my brother with my cell phone. I told him I had arrived at the station and that everything was fine. Then I asked him how work went. He was working two days in my place because the guy I sometimes worked for needed to finish a project that I was helping him with before I left. My brother told me that Carolina's father had called our parents because I hadn't answered my phone when he called me. Then my parents had called my brother because I hadn't answered the phone when they called me. I told my brother that I had turned my phone off during the ride, and I asked him what everybody wanted. He said that Carolina's father wanted to let me know that he left a car outside of the hospital for Carolina and I to use when she was feeling better and allowed to leave the grounds, probably just temporarily at first, he said. My brother said that he was supposed to tell me what it looked like. He said it was a little green hatchback. "Sea green," he said. "A Honda," he said.

"Okay," I said, "thanks." I didn't know why everybody kept calling it a hospital or why I was thinking of it as a hospital myself.

I told my brother I had to go and then said bye. When I hung up the phone, I saw that I was at a pier. I had walked too far, but I didn't care. I walked out on the wooden boards. I was the only person out there. It was windy, and looking out at the water I could see the white tops of the waves, but underneath the pier the water was calmer. I looked down and saw some minnows swimming by. The wind had blown my hair around and I could see it now in my reflection in the water and I tried to fix it. I thought about how Carolina would always say that my hair was too big when it got filled with air. I stayed there for a good half an hour, looking out at the water and down at the minnows, and sometimes fixing my hair in the reflection.

I thought about how I didn't want to live a real life. I wanted to live an imaginary life, but not entirely imaginary in the sense that everything is enclosed in that world. I wanted to think of things and enjoy the thoughts and think about how the things that I was thinking of and enjoying could be done, and I wanted to feel that they actually could or maybe even would be done. But at the same time, I wanted to not ever do anything, and I wanted to think that thought, and know it as a fact, but have it not affect the way I felt about the imaginary life I would have.

I thought about this and about how it was exactly what I wanted. I thought about it all again in my head but with less effort, and it gave me a little energy.

I took my cell phone out of my jacket pocket but then thought that it would probably be hard to hear on the pier, so I walked back towards the street and stepped down the wooden steps. I was going to call Carolina's father but when I got to the street I had momentum so I just kept going.

The hospital was more like a clinic, and it wasn't even that. It was a house. I don't know what I had expected but I guess I had some image of a big new-looking building in my mind, or if not big and new-looking, then at least a building. But this place was more like a house than a building. Like one of those beach houses with ten bedrooms that a bunch of people might get together to split the rent on so it's cheaper and like some kind of big party vacation.

From the street I stared at the front door for a short time before deciding that I didn't want to go in yet, that I wanted to walk around the neighborhood. Since I'd already been out to the pier, I thought I would go the other way, back towards town, and turn in a direction at the first big enough cross street that I came to. I didn't know where I'd go exactly, but I knew that I didn't want to end up where the bus had stopped, just in case it was still there and the driver was still there. I didn't want to have to talk to him again or for him to even see me from a distance and then think things about me inside his head.

I walked with my hands inside my jacket pockets and my eyes pointed down at the ground. I thought about how I must have appeared to a bird or something in the sky high enough up above me to not care about what I was doing.

I slept in the car that first night in the front passenger seat, reclined all the way. At first I was trying to get comfortable in the driver's seat. I tried to maneuver myself around the steering wheel using that lever that allows you to adjust its position. I got it set the best I could and then realized that I didn't have to stay on the driver's side, so I moved over. That was at about eleven o'clock on the first night. The dashboard on the car had a clock that always showed you what time it was, even without the key in it. There was a streetlamp near where I was parked, up high shining light down, so I covered my face with the hood of the sweatshirt that I was using as a blanket over my torso.

In the morning, I went early into her room, which was furnished with a corner wrap bookshelf, a dresser, a desk, and a little nightstand—all from Ikea, all the natural wood color. Carolina was watching *E! True Hollywood Story* about some actress from the eighties.

"Hey," I said.

"Hi," she said in a drawn out manner and then looked back at the television.

"What are you watching?" I said, even though I already knew.

"*True Hollywood Story*, but I'm not really watching it," she said.

"Looks like you're watching it."

"Not really."

"Well then see what's on Discovery or Animal Planet, would you?" I said.

She found Animal Planet on the TV guide channel and turned to it. It was insects. She channeled down and found Discovery. It was *Battle of the Beasts*, this show where they match up animals that wouldn't normally come into contact with one another in real life—a shark and a gorilla, for example. They don't actually match the animals up against one another, just a computerized match-up—a fake fight. Usually the outcome of the battle hinges on habitat, where the fight takes place. They mention that like four or five times in every episode. They say, "hinges on habitat," and I think about the word hinge used in that context and I know what they mean but wonder why they phrase it that way. I end up repeating the term some other time, in speaking about some other thing, and feel stupid for about three seconds and then I don't care.

This particular match-up was a bear versus an alligator. It wasn't even a Grizzly, it was a black bear. I was rooting for him. Carolina knew I'd root for the bear and thought it was boring that she could predict that.

"Bears are mammals, alligators are reptiles," I said.

"Yeah but alligators are basically dinosaurs," she said.

"Yeah, dinosaurs were reptiles."

"Dinosaurs were awesome, is what they were."

I didn't say anything.

On the television, they had a mechanical alligator head simulating the movements of its jaw, demonstrating the power of the down bite. It bent the hell out of a hardened steel pipe and chomped a watermelon into a lot of little pieces. The black bear's bite crushed a reinforced motorcycle helmet, and then his upper arm strength shattered a car's windshield. They had some experts on the show, one for the bear and one for the alligator, who went through all the strengths and weaknesses of each creature. Then they had the final match-up. It was a computerized battle near the water's edge in the Florida Everglades, which favored the alligator. They went to commercials before the fight started. We muted the television and stared at the screen. The first two commercials were for some kind of meat. We talked about how many televisions commercials are about meat and then tried to guess what the next commercial would be. It was for toothpaste. Carolina spoke. She said, "Where are you going to sleep at night?"

"In the car."

"What car? I thought you took the bus."

"Your dad left a car here for us to use. Didn't he tell you?"

"He didn't tell me."

"He told me. He called me but my phone was off so he called my parents and then they called me but it was still off so they called my brother and then when I got off the bus I called him and found all this out."

"You'll sleep in the car? It's cold outside."

"It's not too bad. And I have my sleeping bag."

"Why don't you get a room somewhere?"

"I don't want to spend the money."

"How did you get the keys?"

"There was a spare key in one of those little magnetic boxes that you stick to the undercarriage of your car somewhere. Or in the wheel well or something. It was in the wheel well."

She nodded with her head facing me, but her eyes were on the television screen. It was a commercial for honey.

"Well, I think you should get a room," she said.

"Alright, I'll see what's around."

"And when you do, see if there's any place with good chocolate. The European kind of chocolate. I don't like all the sweetener they add to the chocolate here—makes it too sweet. Like all the Hershey's stuff, or whatever."

"Yeah I know. I'll see what I can find. I'll find you something," I said. She was staring at the television. I watched the light flicker on her face, thought about something, then smiled. "You know, I slept in the car last night."

"What?" she said, after turning to look at me.

"I slept in the car last night," I said again.

"You were here last night?" she said. I laughed, then shrugged my shoulders. She shook her head at me, turned back to the television. It was still commercials. "There are so many commercials," she said, then turned to look at me.

She had a face on.

"What?" I said.

"Why didn't you come in?" she said.

"I don't know. I just didn't. I'm here now though," I said. She stared at me. "It was late, I don't know. It doesn't matter now, anyway."

The program came back on. I pointed to the screen and she turned to it. We left it on mute. The fight began. Nothing happened at first. The contestants were "feeling each other out." We didn't hear them say that, but because of the movements they were making on the screen, and the fact that it was the beginning of the fight, I knew the narrator had said it. Like anytime you watch boxing or hockey or whatever other sport that the athletes are allowed to hit each other in. I said it out loud in a mocking tone. Carolina laughed. "I'd rather see them feeling each other up," she said.

"Are you even allowed to have chocolate in here?" I said.

"What do you mean? I can have whatever I want."

"Alcohol?"

"No, but you know what I mean."

"Chocolate is like alcohol."

"No it isn't, shut up."

"It is to you."

"Shut up."

The alligator hit the bear with his tail and the bear took a few steps back, a little off his balance.

"You can't have any alcohol at all?" I said.

"Well, at least not here in the house. I don't think they care if I have, like, some wine or a beer or whatever, but if I come back all drunk that might be a problem."

The bear swiped at the alligator and missed.

"You're allowed out of the house?" I said.

"Yeah, of course. What are you talking about? I am supposed to have somebody with me though if I go anywhere far. My knee's still pretty sore anyway so I won't be going anywhere far."

They danced around each other for a short while and then the alligator lunged forward and bit down hard on the bear's thigh. The alligator tried to spin but they were on dry land so he didn't do too well. The bear whacked the alligator on the head with his paw and the alligator let go. The bear was bleeding, but it wasn't too bad because he had a lot of protection from fat and thick fur.

"Wait, are you taking medication?"

"Not anymore."

"What do you mean?"

"What?"

"When were you taking medication?"

"No, only at the hospital. Painkillers."

"Oh, okay."

"I'm just here as a kind of relaxation time. Stress free or whatever. Kind of like a vacation."

"Is that what they're calling it?"

The bear stood on his hind legs and roared. We couldn't hear it because the television was still muted. The alligator swiped at the bear with his tail but missed. The bear came forward and the alligator started to run for the water but the bear grabbed him and flipped him over onto his back and sliced open his soft stomach with one swift arm stroke. You could see computer simulated blood and guts pouring out of the computer simulated alligator. That was it for him. The bear tended to his wound as he was named the victor.

Carolina shut the television off and I asked her if she wanted to go for a walk. She said she would like that, so we put on our shoes and headed out of her room.

"Do you have to tell anyone you are going out?" I said.

"No, no. It isn't like that."

"Then this really is like a vacation," I said.

"Shut up," she said.

We walked outside and stopped at the street. Carolina felt cold so we walked to the car and I got her a sweatshirt.

"Hey, this fits me," she said.

"It's a little big."

"Yeah, but it fits me pretty good."

"Yeah."

"Where do you want to go?" she said.

"Down to the pier?"

"Okie-doke," she said.

We were silent on the way down. It was a few minutes' walk. I kept getting ahead of Carolina and then slowing myself down to let her catch up, but without thinking I would get ahead again, so at one point I just stopped moving completely. I looked up past the houses at the sky. It was half blue and half clouds, the puffy ones. I moved my head back slowly as far as it would go until I was almost looking backwards. I saw the sun in the sky right over the top of us, covered by a cloud. I looked at Carolina. She smiled and then looked at me and then smiled again.

"The air is brisk," I said. "It feels good."

"It's fresh," she said.

There was more silence. Only footstep sounds again. Carolina caught up. Then I ran up ahead and turned back towards her saying, "Hey, watch this." I tried to do a handstand but I couldn't get my legs straight up into the air. I let myself fall sideways onto the ground.

"That was weird," she said. She stopped and was standing next to where I was lying on the ground. She hovered over me like a giant, blocking the sun. I looked around, swiveling my head.

"Why'd they send you out here anyway," I said.

"I don't know. Some kind of precaution or something."

"What do you mean?"

"I think some of the doctors thought I was trying to kill myself."

"What?" I said. I stood up and we were facing each other.

"I don't know. I mean, I didn't exactly get out of the way, so they think, well, I don't know what they think. I don't know what was going on."

"Yeah."

"I mean, I wasn't doing anything on purpose. I just sort of froze. I didn't know what was happening. Maybe I could have gotten out of the way. I don't know."

I didn't say anything—only looked at her.

"Maybe it was my pain body."

"Your what?" I said.

"I have a strong pain body according to this book I'm reading. I found it on the shelf in the little library thing in there."

We started walking again towards the ocean.

"What book?" I said.

"Some stupid new age book. I don't believe in any of that, but it's kind of interesting to read in a way."

I didn't say anything. I was looking down at the road, watching my feet touch down and then lift up.

"I'm going to get some money out of this anyway, you know," she said.

"Really?"

"Yeah, but not as much as it could have been. That's why the doctors have been saying that about me being kind of suicidal or whatever. They're all in cahoots. That's why they sent me out here on this vacation. So it could end up being shared liability or whatever. That's it for you. Hospitals, big drug, all the insurances, government. It's all the same stuff."

"Cahoots," I said so that it would come out of my own mouth.

"Yeah, cahoots," she said.

"How much?"

"I don't know. Eighty thousand."

"Eighty thousand dollars?"

"Something like that."

"That's a lot of money."

"What, you want to marry me now?"

"You want to have my baby, don't you?"

"Right now this second."

"You can't just have a baby. You have to make one."

"Well get over here. Quick."

She started unfastening her belt.

"There's some cover over there, we can do it standing. You're a little short but we'll make it."

She started wiggling her jeans down. I laughed.

"C'mon," I said, "cut it out."

"Alright but I don't want to hear you complaining later that I'm not interested. I am ready and willing right here. Let it be known."

"You are not. You are full of it."

"Yeah, yeah, make me full of it."

I walked over to her. She was standing in between two parallel rows of chest high hedges on some absent vacationer's lawn. Right before I got to her, she re-buckled her belt saying, "Nope. Too late now. You missed your chance buster." I put my arms around her and lifted her off the ground, then set her back down. "Wait, do it again," she said, "from the front. Do it right." I wrapped my arms around her, over her arms, and locked my hands together in the middle of her back.

"Ready?" I said.

"Yeah." I arched my back backwards and lifted her off the ground again, shaking her up and down slightly. Her back cracked four times. "Yes," she said, "that was a good one."

I brought her back to land and we walked on towards the ocean. "A couple more back cracks like that and I think we can start to draft up that prenuptial agreement," she said. I laughed.

"Let's just get to the pier first and take a look at that thing," I said.

"What thing?"

"You know, that big thing of water. It's there. We'll see it. We'll look at it, see how we feel," I said. She was looking at me. She turned her head and looked up towards the ocean which we couldn't see past the dunes but knew was there.

"See how we feel," she said, wanting the phrase to come out of her own mouth for some reason.

I spent a few more nights there, all of them in the car except the last one in which I slept with Carolina. We hid me in her closet until she officially went to bed and then I came out, got undressed. It was a small bed but we fit okay. We watched television for a while. I kept turning the volume down and then Carolina would turn it back up. She didn't seem to be worried about us getting caught, but I was, even though it didn't matter. We touched each other and then turned the television off and had sex. In the morning when we woke up, we had sex again and then we ate breakfast. At breakfast Carolina asked when she was being discharged.

"You discharge yourself here," they told her. "You didn't know?"

So, after breakfast, we packed her stuff into the car and I started driving us away from the coast.

"I want to be alive in a good way," Carolina said.

"I know," I said reaching across to touch her shoulder. I reminded myself to pay attention to the road.

"What should we do?" she said. I turned to look at her. She was already looking at me. Then I turned my head back towards the road and concentrated on the dashed lines. I thought about saying something but nothing came out of my mouth.

We went home and the year passed while Carolina tried again to write her thesis—but couldn't—and when she gave up, we decided to leave again. That's when Carolina was going around saying we'd be gone a year or more. We left home and we headed for I-95 South and when we got to it, I realized that I didn't have my passport. We turned around, then decided not to go back for it, and turned around again. We had traffic pretty bad passing around D.C. towards the west. Then there was a long line of cars getting through a row of small towns with too many traffic lights and the engine monitor on the dashboard was showing a very hot temperature. "Here we go," I said pretending to be an astronaut pushing buttons. I shut off the radio and the A.C., rolled down the windows and turned the car heater on full. It wasn't too hot outside, but the sun was shining and that car held the heat pretty well when it was in the sun. We were sweating in the car and Carolina was vocalizing her doubts about the necessity of having the heater on. "It's an old trick," I said, "It brings the engine heat away from the engine."

"I'm dying," she said.

"It's just until we get moving faster again."

"But does it really work?" she said, "I don't think it does anything."

I didn't say anything and then she said, "Let's see what happens if we turn it off, we haven't tried it with it off."

"Alright," I said.

She turned the heater off and rolled her window halfway up. "It's boring enough without the radio on," she said. We moved along that way for a while in silence, neither of us talking. It was stop-and-go and I kept looking at my arm, at the veins in my arm, thinking that I must be a really easy person to draw blood from. I looked back and forth at the road and then the thermometer and then the clock. It always said five-something. After rush hour passed there were fewer cars on the road and we were going faster and the engine was cooling down. Carolina played late-60s British folk rock through the car stereo and I turned the volume up so she could sing along.

Halfway down Skyline Drive we stopped at Big Meadows campground. We drove around the open loops, C, D and E, a couple of times until we found a spot we liked. We got out of the car to walk around a little and then changed our minds and drove to a shadier spot. We pulled in and parked the car and I walked to the ranger station to pay the registration fee: seventeen dollars. When I got back to the campsite, we set up the tent and then cooked dinner on a portable gas stove. I tied a thin rope between two trees near our tent. After dinner we cleaned the kitchen stuff, took showers at the facility center and went to bed. Before bed, I hung the towels and some of our clothes on the rope I'd strung up. While we were lying in the tent, side by side, Carolina asked me if there were bears in this area. "Only black bears," I said, and then a few seconds later, "They're vegetarians."

"No, sometimes they eat meat."

"Okay, but they don't kill it. They don't hunt, I mean. They don't eat people. They might slice you up with their claws but they won't eat you."

"Maybe," she said.

Some time passed in silence. I thought about when I saw a little black bear chasing a fawn across the top of the ridge that you can see from the campsites on the right side of loop H, which was closed now because of a mudslide. The fawn was screaming and zigzagging through the trees awkwardly—limbs moving around like a marionette puppet. It made me think of my grandfather, how he had this gigantic tin of pennies that he would dump out onto the floor and then pick up one by one and put them back inside. That was his version of physical therapy.

"Are you awake?" I said.

"Yes," she said.

"I'm going to say a word and I want you to say the first thing you think of, okay?" I said.

She didn't say anything. I waited. It seemed like a long time.

"You sleepy?" I said.

"Is that the word?" she said.

"No, I mean, that was a real question."

"Oh, I was waiting for the word."

"Okay, um."

There were a few moments of silence and then I said "piano" at the same time she started saying, "I don't really like this tent."

"What?" I said.

"Sorry, give me another word, quick."

"Portobello"

"Mushroom."

I laughed and then she laughed.

"Maybe we should try a different game."

"No, let's do another one," she said.

"Okay," I said. "Um, carrot."

"Are you hungry or something?" she said.

"No, you are supposed to just say the first word you think of."

"Okay, I thought of cake."

I laughed. "Okay," I said.

"Let's try something else," she said.

"Like what?"

"I will think of something and try to send you a picture of it telepathically and you have to tell me what picture I sent you."

"Okay. Go."

"Okay, now, I'm sending now," she said.

I closed my eyes and after a few seconds said, "Wait, I am getting too many images in my head. I don't know how to choose just one. Maybe we should have like a category or something. Like, let's do animals from Africa."

"Okay," she said, "wait." Then she said, "Okay, now, I'm sending it now."

I said, "zebra," and she said, "No, giraffe."

Then I said, "I totally saw a giraffe first but then I saw a zebra more clearly, so I said that."

"You try and send me one," she said.

"What category?" I said.

"States," she said.

"Okay," I said. "Now, I'm sending now."

She said, "Wait, I see the shape. But I don't remember the name—the one with the point at the bottom."

"What?"

"You know, Las Vegas?"

I laughed. "No, it was Minnesota," I said.

"What, no."

"No, I mean the state I was trying to send you was Minnesota."

"Oh," she said. "We're not very good at this."

"We'll get better," I said.

We were quiet for a while and I was almost sleeping. "Nevada," she said, "It's Nevada."

"How could you forget Nevada?" I said.

In the morning we went for a walk in the woods which were misty and chilly. We took pictures with a small digital camera of each of us standing in the mist over a stream. We looked at the pictures after we took them and then took more pictures of us standing over other things like dead logs, fallen trees, and piles of rocks. Then we went back, packed up the campsite and got into the car going south on Skyline Drive out to the bottom of Virginia. Carolina had a friend in Blacksburg who we were going to stop and see on our way past. She called him on my cell phone and then handed it to me. I was driving. "I don't like to talk to him on the phone, I can never understand what he says with that accent," she said.

"I think it's against the law in Virginia to talk on the phone and drive," I said.

"Hello?" the voice on the phone said.

"Hi, Robby?" I said.

"Yeah, who's this?" he said. The way he spoke made me picture flags and guns. I was slow to answer.

"It's Art, Carolina's friend," I said.

"Oh, yeah. Hey man, how's it goin'," he said. "Where are you guys?"

"Good, good, we're, uh, we're on our way out of Shenandoah National Park and coming, coming down past Blacksburg," I said.

"Yeah, yeah, cool, you gonna stop in, I don't know if y'all can stay here but y'all can probly stay over at Fenton's parents' farm, it's not far," he said.

"Alright, well how do we get there?" I said.

"Is Carolina there, can I talk to her?" he said.

I looked at her and made a motion and she shook her head. I said, "Actually we're at a gas station and she's in the bathroom, I thought I'd call for the directions and all."

"They got gas stations in the park?" he said.

"Yeah, a few," I said, "Kind of expensive though."

"What's it runnin' you?" he said.

"Um, like, four-twenty-nine for regular, I think," I said. I looked at Carolina who had a confused expression on her face. I shrugged my shoulders and opened my mouth but didn't say anything.

"A gallon?" Robby said.

"Yeah." I said.

"That's insane," he said.

"Yeah, well, I guess they got you here if you're here," I said.

"Guess so," he said. "Well, alright, you just take the highway across once you get out of the park and—"

"Hold on, I should write this down," I said.

"Just get goin' west outta the park and then gimme a call when you get closer to Blacksburg and I'll tell ya from there, I gotta run now, see ya soon," he said.

"Alright," I said.

Robby's house was a townhouse in one of those complexes of townhouses that all look exactly the same. That's what I said to Carolina when we got there, "These places all look exactly the same." I think a lady on her second floor balcony heard me and felt offended. She flicked her cigarette over the ledge and disappeared.

Robby was an architectural design student at Virginia Tech. Three other people lived in the townhouse with him. The place was messy and Robby said that they had had a party the night before. "Not me though," he said as he was opening a can of Coke, "I don't drink."

"Yeah, I heard that about you," I said.

"You drink that wine stuff?" he said, "I don't know how Carolina drinks that stuff." He was smiling.

"It's good," she said.

"Yeah, I like wine," I said.

We talked for a little while in the common room and met each of Robby's roommates as they came around. They were all architectural design students like him. Robby asked if we wanted anything to drink and we said no. I said no and Carolina looked at me and then said, "Well, no, not right now, thanks."

Robby said, "So, you stayin' the night or what?"

"Well, we're not sure what we're doing," Carolina said.

"We don't really have things planned out," I said.

"Hold on, lemme call Fenton," he said. He took his cell phone out of his pocket and pushed some buttons on it. Then he put it to his ear. "Fenton, Carolina's here," he said. "Yeah," he said. "You comin' over?" he said. "Alright," he said. "Yeah," he said, "bye." He hung up the phone and said, "Fenton'll be here in a minute, he don't live too far."

"Okay," Carolina said. "Hey, can we use your Internet?"

"Yeah, sure," Robby said.

We went into Robby's bedroom and he got out his laptop from under the bed. "Actually, we have a computer with us," I said.

"Oh, yeah, alright," he said, "the account is kingrobby and the password is godgunsglory, all one word." I smiled at him and he just laughed.

We looked on the Internet for campgrounds in Kentucky, which was maybe where we were headed. We didn't find much except for small state parks which we knew to be sometimes nice and sometimes kind of depressing. If you have to go too far off the road to get to them, it isn't really worth it unless you're desperate.

Fenton arrived and greeted Carolina before I was introduced to him. We shook hands and he asked us if we wanted to stay at his parents' farm which wasn't too far away. We said we would and then got his cell phone number and asked for directions to a nearby camping store where we could get some supplies. Carolina wanted to buy a new tent because the one I had brought along was small and didn't keep the moisture out very well. It was a light tent that I had gotten cheap a long time ago at an army surplus store. I was okay with it, but admitted that it wasn't extremely comfortable for the two of us and so I agreed to get a different one even though I didn't really want us to spend money on it. Robby gave us directions to a Dick's Sporting Goods nearby and then told us a story about how his mom wanted to find out if something specific was stocked at Dick's so she went on the computer and typed in "www.dicks.com."

When we were in the car on the way, I said to Carolina, "Did you see the thing he was wearing?"

"Who?" she said.

"Fenton."

"No, what thing, what do you mean?"

"He was wearing one of those W.W.J.D. bracelets."

"What is that?"

"It stands for What Would Jesus Do."

"Oh, really? Weird," she said.

We got to Dick's and found a good tent for a reasonable price. We spent a long time in the store looking at all the options until we finally decided on the tent that I knew we were going to eventually buy and then we bought it. We got back into the car and looked at the map of Virginia and Kentucky. We looked at more maps of the region across the middle: Missouri, Kansas, Colorado. "Maybe we should drive on tonight through Kentucky and across to St. Louis. Do you want to go to St. Louis? It looks like about ten or twelve hours, and there's not really anything for us in Kentucky," I said.

"Yeah, okay," Carolina said. "Let's do that then."

"Alright. Shouldn't we call Fenton and tell him we're just going to drive on?"

"Can you call him?"

"I don't even know him. You know him."

"Not really."

"Alright, give me the phone."

"You have it."

I called Fenton and told him that we weren't going to stay at his parents' farm because we thought we needed to get out west at a quicker pace. He said he understood and that if we were ever back through that way, we should call him up. The way his voice was projected made him sound like a counselor or a therapist. While noticing that, I realized that when we'd shaken hands, he had used both hands in the way that church pastors sometimes do. I said "thanks" and "will do" and then we hung up. Carolina thanked me and I said something about how it was all okay.

I looked at the map for a little while and then turned on the car and drove it through some small country roads out of Virginia and then onto the highway heading west. It was dark and the roads were winding around through wooded areas and I felt a little bit sleepy. I was unsure if we were going the right way but I kept driving, followed signs, turned around a couple of times, and then followed more signs. Carolina got some things from the cooler that was now in the back seat and made us sandwiches. We ate them in the dark as I drove us through the night, everything calm and away from us.

I drove all night while Carolina slept upright in the passenger seat with her eyes shut and her mouth open. It was funny to watch. Her head rolled back and forth with the road. I didn't have the radio on. I just sat there for hours with the sound of the engine and the tires and thought about how we had no idea what we were doing—how it was just easier to be alive this way, going to new places, moving a lot. What we wanted was for things to happen to us, to not be in control. We wanted a different kind of life, one that would come to us if we just gave it the chance. We had gotten our hands on some money, so we could afford it.

A few miles outside of St. Louis, early in the morning, I pulled into a rest stop and slept for an hour. I shut the car off but forgot the lights, so when I woke up and tried to turn the car on, it wouldn't start. It was chilly out ... still dark, just before dawn. While running up to the building to see if I could find someone with jumper cables, I thought, "It's always darkest right before dawn," and then shook my head at myself for thinking that. I asked a man emptying the trashcans if they had jumper cables around but he just looked at me, shook his head, and said, "Polish." In the light of the sidewalk lamp, he seemed like a small wax figure version of someone my dad used to know named Lazlo. I went around the other side of the building to the gas station and got them to come over to the car with a little battery machine. They jumped the car, charged me ten bucks, and then we were ready to go. I left the car running, went inside, urinated, got a coffee, and then came back out and drove us into St. Louis with piano blues playing on the car stereo. There almost wasn't anybody on the highway.

We found a park and slept in the grass with our socks and shoes off. When we got hungry we woke up and took the car for something to eat. It started up just fine. I had eggs and potatoes and Carolina ate blueberry pancakes. The day was getting on near afternoon by the time we were finished, so we found a cheap motel to stay at on the edge of the city. It wasn't exactly a nice place, but it was clean and we had a bathroom to ourselves. We took showers and then drove into town. We didn't know anything about St. Louis, which turned out to seem like a really quiet place—in a good way, or at least in a way that I liked. We found this weird museum full of stuff that was made entirely from recycled materials. We spent a couple of hours in there. I don't really know what we saw, or what even happened inside the museum, but I remember an "Alien Elvis Baby," whatever that is, and we made finger paintings of each other's profiles which we just left there on the drying racks.

When we left the museum, we walked around the city not knowing where to go and not caring too much. We talked about Robby and Fenton. "They are real Southerners, aren't they?" Carolina asked.

"Yeah, they are definitely from Virginia," I said.

"Is it the Bible Belt there or what? I've never understood where that place is supposed to be." Carolina said.

"Well, I don't really think it's a place. I think it's deeper south, but I'm not sure. I don't really know."

"What was with that bracelet then?"

"I don't know."

"Do you think he doesn't drink alcohol because of the bracelet thing?"

"I don't know. But anyway wasn't that Robby who doesn't drink?"

"Oh right," Carolina said, "then I don't know."

Neither of us said anything for a while. We were becoming tired from walking so much and not sleeping very well. "Do you want to go back to the motel?" I asked.

"I guess so," Carolina said.

"I feel kind of tired."

"Okay, let's go and rest or something," she said.

When we got there we went inside and turned the television on. We felt something that we called negative energy. I don't know if I felt the negative energy by myself or if I felt it because Carolina felt it and passed it on to me across the bed, but I think she probably passed it to me and I maybe resented her a little bit for it, even though I was being ridiculous.

"Let's go for a walk," I said after fifteen or twenty minutes of channel surfing.

"I'm tired of walking," Carolina said.

"Do you want to take the car somewhere?" I asked.

"We just got back here."

"Yeah, I know. I don't know," I said.

"I don't know. Where do you want to go?" Carolina asked.

"Let's look on the Internet."

"No, I don't feel like turning it on and everything."

"Okay," I said and stared at a strange hole in the wall across from me, high up near the ceiling. I didn't know what to say so I brought her attention to the hole. "What's that hole?" I asked.

"What hole?"

"Up there near the ceiling," I said, and got up, walked towards it—pointing at it. Carolina got up and stood next to me. We stood on our tiptoes and squinted our eyes trying to understand what the hole was. Then I sat down on the bed and then lay down and looked at the ceiling. My legs were hanging off the end of the bed with my knees bent around it. I turned my head sideways and looked at the curtains on the window and then the window itself and then I looked out of it. From that distance I couldn't see much, just colors really, but from the colors I was able to determine what was out there. Nothing unusual: tree, car, building, sky.

"Let's just drive to a part of town we didn't walk in," Carolina said, puffing the words.

"Alright," I said, "let's go."

"I have to go to the bathroom first."

"Okay," I said, and looked at the hole again while hearing the empty metallic sound of Carolina urinating in the bathroom with the door open.

We drove down south from the center of the city. I parallel parked the car and we got out and stood leaning against it. We picked a street and walked along it. All of the shops were closed. Carolina looked in the windows at displays of shoes. We saw a sign for a chocolate bar and walked a little faster to it, but it was closed. Carolina started walking away and I stopped. I said, "Hey, what time is it?"

"I don't know," she said.

"It says here this place opens at five-thirty," I said. I took out my cellphone and looked at the time. "That's in twelve minutes."

We walked around the corner and sat down in the shade on the curb of a green lawn. A few cars went by but there wasn't much traffic. We knew that in about twelve minutes we were going to get up and go to the chocolate bar, even though we hadn't verbally decided on it.

"Everything feels a little fucking fucked right now," Carolina said.

"Fucking fucked," I said, wanting it to come out of my own mouth. I looked at a bird on a tree branch and said, "I know. I feel it too. But let's just be calm, like that bird." The bird seemed to be looking right at my face.

"I don't know. I feel nervous," she said.

"Soon we can eat chocolate," I said.

Carolina looked at me and then put her fingers into my hair and made twirling motions. "When you play with your hair, it gets all straight and ugly," she said, "I have to re-curl it."

I didn't say anything. Then I said, "Hey, how many people do you think are eating chocolate right now?"

"In the world?"

"Yeah, in the world."

"In what form, like a chocolate bar?"

"I don't know. In any form. How many people are eating some form of the cocoa bean right now?"

"You mean the actual bean?"

"Come on, seriously, just take a guess."

"I hate it when you ask me these mathematical questions."

"This is not a mathematical question. A mathematical question is like what is thirteen times twenty-nine."

"This is like a math word problem, then."

I laughed.

"If Jane left Chicago on a train heading east at ninety miles per hour and Mark left Pittsburgh on a train heading west at seventy-five miles per hour, where will they meet?" Carolina asked.

"That is a bad word problem. You don't give enough information. You have to at least say how far Chicago is from Pittsburgh. Or something," I said. "Wait, no, you need even more information than that."

"Whatever, I hate word problems," she said.

"I like them," I said.

"What time is it?" she said.

"Is this a trick question?" I said.

"Shut up. Give me the phone."

I looked at the clock on my phone. It said 5:37. "We can go now," I said.

I got up from the curb and gave Carolina my hands so she could pull herself up. We moved our legs and carried our bodies around towards the street where the chocolate bar was. We got there, went in and walked to a table in the garden out back. We sat down across from each other and looked at each other. There was no one else out there.

"Did they see us come in?" Carolina said. "Do you think they know we're here?"

"Don't worry," I said.

"I'm not worrying, I just don't know if they know we're here."

"Who would go to Pittsburgh anyway?" I said.

"I would," she said.

"No you wouldn't," I said.

"I've been there. It's nice. They have rivers and stuff," she said.

I laughed, looked at the menu. "What do you want?" I asked.

She looked at me strangely and then said, "Nothing, leave me alone."

"What?" I asked, and looked at her. "I mean to order. From the menu." I held the menu up in the air and moved it a little bit.

"Oh," she said, "what do I want from the menu. Um, maybe a truffle or this triple fudge with caramel thing, or wait, maybe something with coconut. Is there like a sampler thing with a lot of stuff on one plate?"

"We could probably ask for something like that," I said.

"They don't even know we're out here," she said.

We ended up ordering three things to eat and two glasses of raspberry Belgian beer. We ate the chocolate and drank the beer and then I paid the bill with my credit card. We stayed for a long time there out back in the garden after paying, not leaving, and when we finally did leave, we walked around the streets a little bit in the dark because we didn't really want to go back to the motel, but then we did go back. We drove back to the motel and went to sleep. Before we went to sleep I watched the television a little. I watched the Discovery channel. There was a show about the evolution of the world. Creatures were just beginning to come onto land from out of the sea for the first time. I watched them wiggling around. I turned the volume on the TV down very low, but not inaudible. I put the sleep timer on thirty minutes and looked at the deadbolt, then the ceiling. Carolina moved her body closer to mine and held my arm against her chest. My eyes stayed open for a while and then they closed. I trusted the sleep timer to turn the TV off when it was supposed to.

In the morning I had an erection that Carolina found by moving her hand along my leg. She touched me while we were still in bed. After a while I said, "Wait, wait," and she said, "No, it'll be fun."

We got up, cleaned ourselves, packed our things, ate cereal and checked out of the motel. We did it slow so that it took the rest of the morning. We were supposed to be out by eleven but we got out at nearly twelve. We drove on west towards Denver. I was driving. I always drove.

We went across into Kansas and had to stop for a ticket from the tollbooth. "I didn't think they had toll roads off the coasts," I said. We stopped at the first rest stop and looked at the map. We looked at alternate routes because Kansas was long and the toll was going to be a lot. We decided that we didn't have a choice, which we felt bad about, so we sat on a wooden picnic table and drank tea with the loud sounds of the highway very close. We boiled the water in a hand-held camping stove with a small propane tank. We drank the tea out of mugs that we'd gotten at a thrift store in St. Louis. Carolina's mug was cylindrical and white with a large handle and had an image of a snake all straight and tight-like suspended over a rock. Below the snake was written, "RELAX." I thought it was funny the way relax was written in all capitals. Reading it made me feel the opposite of relaxed, but the joke itself was nice and calm and the mug looked clear and sharp and like Gary Larson had made it. I liked that mug. The mug I drank out of was gray, also cylindrical with a large handle, and it had an engraved image of white tennis shoes and below them the name Evelyn. When I chose it, Carolina had said, "Evelyn is a girl's name."

"That's why it's funny," I said.

She laughed and said it wasn't funny.

I said, "But you're laughing. And also, what about Evelyn Waugh? He was a man."

"Who is Evelyn Waugh?" she asked.

"Oh, he was an English writer. Or he was American and English or something. I'm not sure. Anyway, he wrote *The Loved One*."

"What's it about?" she asked.

"The main character works at a pet funeral home and he likes this girl who ends up dying. I forget."

"Sounds dark."

We finished drinking the tea and got back on the highway. After a few miles of driving, there was another tollbooth. We paid a couple of bucks and then drove off toll-free into the middle of Kansas. That was enough to make us feel good. We put the windows down and listened to something loud on the stereo. I reached behind me and rolled the back window down a little so that the air would flow better past my head and bother my hair less. Carolina did the same. We looked at each other and held hands between the seats.

"Where should we sleep tonight?" I asked.

"I don't know. Let's not think about it now," she said.

I said okay and kept us moving at a constant speed, slowing down a little if we went by a place where it looked like a cop might be hiding.

Later it was dark and we were alone on the highway. There was a lightning storm far off in the distance that we watched long before we came to it. We saw flashes of light all across the horizon from left to right. Soft acoustic music was coming out of the stereo and Carolina used the digital camera to take videos of the storm. The closer we got, the more the lightning wrapped around us until eventually we started seeing flashes coming from everywhere, even behind us. We saw some sharp bold streaks of light which made Carolina flinch. "I'm a little worried," she said. "It is really flat out here, we are like the tallest thing."

"It's alright," I said. "The car is grounded by rubber tires so we are safe enough." I didn't know how true that was, but thought I'd heard something about it before.

"Safe enough," Carolina said.

"We're fine," I said. "Besides, there's nowhere we can go that would be safer, so we are where we are." Carolina bounced her leg up and down on the ball of her foot.

"The car can't conduct electricity into us because the tires don't let the circuit complete," I said. I was saying things that seemed to be calming Carolina, though, so I kept talking. "There are no trees to fall on us, so the only thing that could happen is the engine being struck but the likelihood of that is very slim. Plus there are rubber tubes and hoses all through it anyway, so it's okay." I paused a few moments, then continued. "Besides, the storm isn't even on us yet, that lightning is still off on the edges. We might not even pass through it. It's hard to tell where anything really is because it's so flat you just see everything."

I sat up in my seat and drove a little more attentively. Carolina didn't say anything. She was looking out the window to her right and I couldn't see her face. I said, "When you see a streak of lightning, start counting the seconds until you hear thunder. Each second is worth a mile and that's how far away the storm is." She tried on the next bolt and counted fourteen seconds.

"It can't be that far away," she said.

"Maybe each second is a half mile."

"Still not possible."

"Yes it is," I said. "It's scientific."

Ten minutes later we were in the middle of the storm and rain was coming down on us hard and fast. Carolina kept telling me to slow down and I kept saying that everything was okay. The rain got so hard that I couldn't see anything, so I slowed down a lot and put my hazard lights on. Carolina was nervous but we got out of the heavy rain soon and I put my hand on her hand.

When we got out of the rain completely, Carolina moved into the back seat so that she could watch the lightning from out of the back window. While she was moving, her knee hit the gear shift into D2 but I put it back to D and held it there until she had finished moving.

We found a place to camp just off the highway. It was completely empty. The bathrooms were locked and it was too dark to see what was around, even with the high beams on. We had a bad feeling, and were still slightly worried about the storm. We didn't know which direction it was moving. If it was coming towards us—small chance that there was for that—we didn't want to have to pass it again, especially this time in a tent. We got back in the car and drove towards the eastern outskirts of Denver. It was very late when we got to a town so we just took the first motel we came to. We passed a couple of chain hotels to get there, but motels were always cheaper. The room we got was dirty and smelled unclean. We kept our shoes on right up until getting into bed, after inspecting the sheets, and even while using the bathroom.

We slept and left early in the morning without eating breakfast or taking showers. We parked outside of a Best Western, on the street, and used our laptop, stealing the wireless Internet, to find a good breakfast place in Denver which wasn't too far away. The parking lot was full of snow when we got there. We drove around the city trying to understand where we were going. We parked somewhere downtown and walked in the cold and snow to the street where the breakfast place was, but the breakfast place was closed because of the weather. When we were getting out of the car to walk there, Carolina tried to find her scarf, but she couldn't find it anywhere because we were completely unprepared for snow-cold weather. Her neck was cold and the breakfast place was closed and we didn't know where to go or what to do. We stood on the street. People walked past us. Eventually we walked back to the car and got in. I had started walking when Carolina said, "Where are you going?"

"I don't know," I said, "Back to the car?"

We started driving. I think we felt confused. I was the one driving. I'd done all the driving. I decided that I didn't like Denver and Carolina agreed with me. We left Denver and went north to Boulder, Colorado, which wasn't far away. When we got to Boulder it wasn't snowing anymore. Leaving Denver on the expressway I'd thought, "Denver, the last dinosaur. He's your friend and a whole lot more."

I sang it and Carolina said, "Have you ever seen the Italian version?"

I laughed and said, "No, why, is there one?"

"Yeah," she said, "It's funny, the theme song is totally different," and then she hummed the tune.

"Where did you see the Italian version of *Denver the Last Dinosaur*?" I asked.

"On the Internet," she said.

"On the Internet," I said.

In Boulder we found a coffee shop and got hot tea and used wireless Internet for free. I ate a scone, although I didn't say the word scone even when I was ordering it, I just pointed. I said, "I'll have that."

Carolina hit me on the arm and said, "We'll have two scones, please."

After staying in the coffee shop for a while, Carolina felt that we'd stayed as long as we should, so we left and walked around in the streets. My cell phone rang and I looked at it. "It's my uncle," I said.

"Answer it," Carolina said.

"Uncle Wim," I said.

"Hey Arrr-thur," he said. "How's it going? Where are you guys?"

"We're in Boulder, Colorado," I said. We talked for a few minutes and then my aunt wanted to say hi. She asked me how it was going and I said everything was great. She said we had gotten out to Colorado pretty quickly. I said that I'd driven two times for ten hours or more to do it. Then she said that they couldn't find their Home Depot credit card and asked if I still had it. I looked in my wallet, which was just my driver's license, ATM card, and credit card with a rubber band wrapped around them, and found it. I said, "Yeah, I have it. I forgot to give it back, I guess. Sorry. I'll mail it."

"No, no, it's fine, we don't need it. We just wanted to make sure that we hadn't lost it," she said. "Actually, you know what? Why don't you guys go out to dinner tonight and pay for it with the card?"

"Oh, thank you," I said, "but I don't think they take the Home Depot credit card at restaurants."

She laughed. "Yeah, you're right, I wasn't thinking about what it actually was."

Then she said, "Well, you know what, go out to dinner tonight and it'll be on us. I'll give some money to your parents and they can put it into your bank account."

"Okay, that would be great," I said. "Thank you much, we appreciate it."

Carolina was looking at me with a strange contorted face. "They're giving us money to go out to dinner," I said to her.

"Don't mention it," my aunt said.

"What?" I asked.

"You're welcome," she said. "Alright, well, we'll let you lovies go, then. Keep in touch."

"Will do," I said. "Say bye to Uncle Wim."

"I will," she said, "Bye."

"Bye," I said and then hung up the phone. I handed it to Carolina and she put it inside her bag.

"So where do you wanna go to eat?" I asked.

"I don't know," she said. "Let's look around."

"There's got to be a good Indian place in this town," I said.

We found a Nepalese restaurant and made a reservation for eight thirty. While I was making the reservation, Carolina picked up a piece of paper from a stack on a table in the waiting section of the restaurant. "There's a Zen Center," she said. I looked at the piece of paper. I took it out of her hand to read it. She picked up another one.

"Why are you getting another one?" I asked.

"You took the one I was reading," she said.

"Here," I said, giving the flyer back to her.

"No, I don't want it now, whatever," she said.

She walked out of the restaurant lobby and down along the street. I followed after her. "Carolina," I said. She did not answer or look back at me. I walked faster and then she walked faster. She walked across the street to the left side and then walked back across. Then she walked into a supermarket and bought a smoothie in a bottle. She paid for it and then drank it on a bench near the exit and I sat next to her.

"What's wrong?" I asked.

"Why do you have to be so aggressive?"

"What do you mean? I wasn't being aggressive."

"Whatever, fine."

"Look, I'm sorry, I didn't mean to upset you," I said.

She didn't say anything. She stared at the floor.

"Can we just start walking? Can we walk somewhere?" I asked.

"There's nowhere to go," she said.

"What are you talking—okay, let's just start going."

"Where?"

"I don't know, to the Zen Center."

"We don't know where it is."

"It's right over there on the parallel street."

"We'll never find it."

"What are you—yes we will, come on, let's go. I'm going."

I walked out of the supermarket, spotted a perpendicular street and started walking towards it. Carolina followed me slowly. She would stop and look at things in shop windows and then I would get ahead of her and when I would look back I would stop moving until she started moving again.

I thought about the other times this kind of thing had happened and I wondered if it would keep happening for the rest of my life. I thought about how the rest of my life was probably fifty years and that seemed like a long time. I made some calculations in my head and decided that I would probably die in the year 2067. Then I thought about how I eat pretty well and that I'm kind of small which means my heart doesn't have to work too hard to pump blood throughout my body, so I changed the year to 2071. "It will be nice to see what the seventies are like," I thought and laughed.

Eventually Carolina and I ate dinner at the Nepalese restaurant. The food was good and we slept well afterward.

Crossing the Rockies wasn't easy on the car, but we made it into Utah and started going south along the border. We stopped to eat lunch at a rest stop that went down off the highway towards a stream going through the canyons. We took turns using the bathroom while the other stayed with the food that we'd laid out on a parking lot picnic bench, and then we ate. While we were eating I looked at the stream going through the rocks and thought of a song from a John Wayne movie.

> *Purple light in the canyon*
> *That's where I long to be*
> *With my three good companions*
> *My rifle, my pony and me*

Back on the highway, after lunch, Carolina was taking videos of the landscape through the car window. I drove us down towards Arches National Park, which was filled up when we got there. We tried to reserve a campsite for the next day but they didn't take reservations during the off-season, the ranger said. "I'll pay for it in full right now," I said.

"Sorry," he said. "Can't do it."

His mouth moved like a cartoon's mouth. I stared at him saying nothing and then looked at Carolina.

"Just come back tomorrow before two. There should be spots then," he said.

"Alright," I said. Then I drove past the booth, turned around, and went out the exit. I stopped the car before putting it back on the road, and we looked at the map. Back up from where we came was Canyonlands National Park, but they didn't have running water there because it was a bunch of miles off the highway into the middle of the desert, and Carolina wanted to take a shower. We decided to go anyway. It was getting late in the afternoon, so I drove fast. Canyonlands was full too, which made us rethink our current "no-plans, have-no-clue-what-we're-doing" lifestyle as we drove back towards civilization. It was almost dusk when we found a group of roadside campsites, so we weren't too particular about the one we chose.

After setting up the new tent for the first time, we cooked dinner in the dark and then I cleaned the dishes sparingly with drinking water. In the morning we packed up and got out early. I held up a blanket while Carolina urinated near a dry little desert bush.

Arches was still full when we got there. I talked to the same ranger about the same situation using most of the same words. I think he was pretending not to remember me. "We won't know what sites will become vacant until later, if any," he said.

"When? I asked.

"Won't know till we know," he said.

"Okay," I said, and then made the exact same movements with the car that I'd made the day before. Then out near the road we stopped to look at the map again, like before. I decided we should go back to Canyonlands to wait, so I got us back on the road and moving.

"I don't want to go back there," Carolina said.

"There's nothing else around," I said.

"I need a bathroom to get clean. Woman stuff," she said.

"Alright, well, what should we do?" I asked. I had stopped the car and turned around already.

I pulled into a gas station and parked. Carolina got out and walked towards the road. She stopped and stood by it. I sat in the car looking at her in the mirror. Then I went to get her.

"Let's just go," I said. "It's okay."

"I wish you weren't so worried about what will happen," she said.

"I'm not worried," I said. "I don't give a damn."

"Yes, you do."

"Only because it matters to you."

"Nothing matters to me," she said.

"Well, what about this? What about now? It matters."

"I'll take care of myself. If I need a hotel room, then I will pay for it and get it."

"Hey, it's not like that. You've just got to tell me when those things are a factor. When you feel like you need that,"

I said. She didn't say anything. "Come on," I said, and we started walking back towards the car. I filled us up with gas and started driving south towards Moab.

"I looked on the map—we can go to Moab. It's supposed to be a little bit of an alternative town. It's close," I said.

"Okay," she said.

"Do you want to drive?" I asked.

"Actually, yeah I do," she said. "That might be nice."

I stopped the car where I could and then we switched spots. I got out of the car and walked around while Carolina slid across the seats. It was the first time she drove since we'd left, and she'd never actually seen the desert before, so it was the first time she drove herself through the desert.

In Moab we found a cafe where we could get something to drink and use the Internet. We had good fruit smoothies and found a place where we could do laundry. We spent a couple of hours at the laundromat and then decided to get a motel in Moab and stay the night. It was still early in the day because we'd left Canyonlands about an hour after sunrise. There was some kind of Jeep convention happening which had a lot of the motels and hotels booked up, but we found a room in a motel where John Wayne used to stay. I forget the name of it. While Carolina was taking a shower, I lay on the bed and looked at the ceiling. I wondered if John Wayne had slept in the room I was in. I wondered if he'd had sex in the bed, or kept whiskey under it, or something.

We watched a little television and then took a walk around town. Carolina looked around at weird shops and we ended up buying a little pink rock that you're supposed to feel vibrate slightly while holding it in the palm of your hand. I didn't believe it at first, but then I felt it. We walked back to the motel holding hands with the rock in-between.

We made love on the bed and then dinner and then looked at the maps to see where we were going in the morning. "The Painted Desert," I said.

"Which Indian tribes are here?" she asked, pointing at the center of New Mexico.

"Mostly the Hopi, I think," I said. "Did you know that the Hopi say that their gods led them to the desert to escape evil?"

"Really?"

"I think so. And also, no one is allowed to photograph them or their dwellings or anything. It is against their beliefs. So leave your camera in the car. Actually, hide it."

We were silent for a while on the bed, not ready to get inside of it yet. The bedspread was maroon—same as the wallpaper.

"What evil are we escaping?" Carolina asked.

"I don't know," I said. "But something."

Crossing the desert, we were hot enough to wear damp towels that we stole from the John Wayne motel. We wet them and then wrapped them around our heads. We went through Hopi lands and saw some old cliff dwellings from a distance through one of those giant binocular machines that they have on piers to look at the whales.

We decided to go up through Las Vegas and then west to Death Valley. It was dusk as I drove past Phoenix and a lot later than that when we made it to Vegas. We got a room at the Econolodge. They didn't have a casino, but were right next to one, and the motel was cheaper. On the way into town, down the strip, we passed a lot of wedding chapels. We pointed them out and laughed about them. We said, "Now is our chance to get married hassle-free."

We ordered pizza in the motel room after making love. When the delivery guy came, Carolina was still naked. She ran into the bathroom, grabbing her clothes on the way. I stopped her and said, "No, leave them," and I quickly threw them around the room.

"You're so vain," she said. She was smiling. I motioned for her to hide and she went into the bathroom. I opened the front door, paid for the pizza, and closed the door. It was just us two again. I heard her in the bathroom singing, "I bet you think this song is about you."

"It's safe," I said, but nothing happened. I walked towards the bathroom. I heard, "Don't you? Don't you? Don't you?"

When she came out, we ate and laughed, not really talking or doing anything. We didn't have the television on or books out. We just existed in a kind of absence of weight that we hadn't felt in a while. Later, when we were lying in bed, after we'd been there a while with the lights off, Carolina asked, "How did the desert make them safe from evil?" It took me a few seconds before I knew what she was talking about.

"They say that it's because it's a hard life living in the desert," I said.

"And …"

"And historically, for them, whenever they were in a situation where they could have an excess, or things in abundance, then evil started to come to them."

"What do you mean?"

"Like, in the desert they had to work hard just to have just enough of what they needed. They had no excess, no luxuries, only what they needed, and they appreciated it. They had to work hard to get it and it meant something to them. It's more complex than this, but basically, yeah."

"So the desert saved them because it made life harder?"

"Yeah, basically. I mean, I understand it perfectly. It's easier when life is harder. I mean, when you don't have what you need, or barely what you need, then all you care about is getting what you need. Maybe not easier, but simpler. More basic. It's like Maslow's Hierarchy."

"What do you mean?"

"There are different levels, or stages, of existence in which you only move on to the next level when the previous level has been satisfied," I said. She didn't say anything so I continued talking. "Like on the first level, you have the need for water, food, air to breathe. Until you have all of those things, you don't care about anything else. You don't care about the second level. Then when you have water and food, you move on to caring about the next level, which is safety. Then comes love, acceptance, sense of belonging, I think. After that is self-esteem and then after that is understanding things, the world, yourself, *et cetera*."

"No, I know what Maslow's Heirarchy is, I just don't understand what you meant because they did all the top levels as well—they made art, we saw it."

"No, yeah, they made art. I mean, wait, I'm confusing it. I guess it just made me think of Maslow. The Hopi escaped evil by going to the desert because there they could not have more than what they needed. They could have just what they needed. Things were more balanced. They could be in harmony with nature. Balance and harmony with nature were very important to the Hopi. But yeah, they made art."

"Those things are important to us too," Carolina said.

"Yeah," I said.

"I'm glad we have what we need," she said.

"Do we?" I asked.

"I have you," she said. We moved closer together and lay still. My leg was arched over and resting on top of Carolina's legs. "Do you want to be Hopi?" she asked.

"Tomorrow," I said.

"Okay," she said.

"Tonight I want to be us," I said.

"Good," she said.

"Goodnight," I said.

"Goodnight."

In the morning we went north out of Vegas into the middle of nowhere. It was pleasant driving, not too hot yet. I noticed we were into our reserve gas and I was a little worried but mostly amused. I didn't care if we ran out of gas on the highway, but we didn't. We found a station, filled up, and then headed west into California. We traveled a long time on a long flat road with no lines painted on it and we didn't realize we'd entered Death Valley National Park until we saw signs for Zabriskie Point. We found the only campground open and took a long time choosing a campsite. Once I paid the fee and we had our tent set up, we started on foot towards Zabriskie Point and then came back and took the car. We didn't stay long there because it was full of people taking pictures from every possible angle, so we drove to the sand dunes from that movie, Zabriskie Point. There's a scene with many naked couples rolling around in the dunes having sex. It's the famous scene. We walked around in the dunes in the one hundred degree temperature and then found a general store where we could buy some fresh things and something cold to drink.

It was too hot to make a fire and there were mosquitoes everywhere, so we went into the tent after dinner before it was really dark. We lay there for a long time, uncomfortable in the heat, but feeling okay. We were mostly naked on top of our sleeping bags. We read and talked and felt good about not knowing or caring what would happen tomorrow. When it was very dark, I took the rain guard off of the tent and we looked at the stars through the mesh netting. It was an alright tent. It was heavy, but good, and since we had the car, heavy didn't matter. The night took its time getting on late, but we didn't care.

In the morning a while later, eating continental breakfast downstairs from our motel room, we heard about the shootings from a little television high up in the corner above the waffle maker. I was pouring ready-batter and spinning the handle when the TV said there were over twenty people dead, most of them students. I heard it in the background, not giving it much attention, trying to decide whether or not I really wanted to put this waffle in my stomach. Carolina asked me to make her a waffle and I said she could have some of mine. Then she asked me to get juice and I said I already got it. "Get me some juice, then, please," she said. When I found the table she was sitting at she saw me carrying the juice and said, "No, I want the red one."

"They don't have a red one," I said. "Only this one."

"Okay," she said, "is there pulp?"

"What?"

"You know, pulp."

"No, I don't know."

"You don't know what pulp is?"

"I don't."

"The stupid little pieces of stuff."

"Oh, yeah, I think so," I said, "Here, try it."

I was playing dumb because I didn't want to be talking. When we woke, I'd wanted to do it but Carolina was too hungry. "I am so hungry," she'd said. "Let's go down to eat." I got dressed and ready, but real slowly. She just stared out the window down into the parking lot.

We were eating in silence, except for Carolina asking meaningless questions about the quality of the food. "How are the potatoes?"

"I'm surprised there even are potatoes," I said. I was watching the television. Now the volume was off and the captions were on—some guy in a hat did it—but I didn't mind because it gave me an excuse to stare at the TV.

"What is it?" she said.

"Another school shooting," I said.

"High school?"

"No, college, I think, this time."

"Where?"

"Um, I don't think they said."

"What happened?"

"Some kid shot some other kids," I said.

"Did they get him?"

"I think he shot himself too."

Neither of us said anything for a few minutes.

Then, "Oh my god," I said.

"What?" she asked as she turned around in her seat to look at the television. "I don't have my glasses on," she said. "Where are my glasses?"

"It was Virginia Tech," I said.

"Oh my god," she said and got out of her chair and walked closer to the television.

"Did they say who was killed?"

"They aren't identifying them yet," I said, already knowing what she was going to say next. "But they weren't engineering students. English students, I think."

"Because you know—" she said.

"Yeah, I know," I said, cutting her off. She came back to the table and sat down. We made eye contact briefly and I continued eating. We weren't talking. I was thinking about the waffle, still wondering if I wanted to be eating it, chewing away. There was syrup all over my lips and when I tried to wipe it off the napkin stuck. "I need water," I said. "Running water—going to the bathroom."

"In the room?" she asked.

"No, there's one in the hall there, be right back."

I washed my face and looked at myself in the mirror. I went back to the table and Carolina was eating the waffle. "You're gonna need to wipe that syrup off before it's too late," I said. I sat down and didn't do anything.

After a little while Carolina said, "I can't believe we were there. Of all the schools in the country."

"Yeah," I said.

"Do you think Robby is all right?" she asked.

"Yeah," I said, "I do."

❖

Some time later, after we found out who he was and what exactly had happened, we had an odd conversation. It was because I said that violent actions had an important function in society. Carolina was making a face. "Are you serious?" she said. I didn't really care about any of this, didn't know why I was in the conversation, or why I'd started it.

"No," I said, "But, I mean, it is an interesting point of view."

"What are you talking about?"

"I don't really believe in it, but I partially believe in it," I said.

"In what?" she said.

"I don't know."

"What?"

"Look, I don't know," I said. "Forget it, I'm just tired."

"Okay," she said, but she didn't seem satisfied.

"It's just the Marxist view I'm talking about. The idea that things have to get really bad for people to know there's a problem."

"Like how we always say it's going to be with factory farming, you mean."

"In a way, yeah. I mean, it's already happening. Mad Cow Disease and all that other stuff. It will get worse and then, in theory, it will get so bad that a giant, almost immediate change will take place."

"I don't think that's going to happen."

"Maybe not," I said.

"But even if it did, how is a school shooting like that?"

"I guess it's like that because when people hear about it they pay attention."

"I guess," she said.

"I mean, this guy, he wrote literature, right? He wrote plays and stories and they were pretty disturbing to a lot of people but no one really paid all that much attention to it. Maybe one or two people."

"Yeah, but his literature wasn't, like, successful. So a lot of people couldn't have read it. They didn't know it existed."

"Okay, but think about, like, a best selling novel. If you write a novel and it becomes a best seller—one million copies sold—then that's not even one percent of people in America that have read your book."

"And?"

"And, if you kill twenty people and then yourself, well, then a lot more people are affected by your message."

"You think a rampage like this is a message?"

"Isn't it?"

"I guess so."

"All I'm saying is that I can understand the point here."

"Which is what?"

"Which is that an—an act of terror, while tragic, can also serve a purpose."

"What purpose?"

"I don't know. We're going to have to talk about this another time, when I can explain what I mean, because right now I can't," I said.

"Okay."

"Let's just forget about it. Can we do that?"

"Sure."

We walked into town. I looked at Carolina's face from the side and I didn't say anything. I thought about other ways I could explain what I had been trying to say. I thought of other arguments, other analogies, but I decided against saying them. I looked up at the sky and watched the clouds above the buildings. When Carolina looked in the windows of shops, I stopped with her and waited without hurrying. She pointed at things and said words and I looked and made noises. After a long time it got dark and we were still walking.

TWO

The Ski Lodge

We went back home again, confused about what to do and heavy with a lot of energy that we didn't know how to place. This was something like the fourth time, leaving and coming back. On the way into town, just across the bridge, Carolina made these random high-pitched sounds with her mouth and I moved my eyes around in circles a few times real fast.

Carolina's grandmother had died while we were gone and a sub-letter was living in our apartment so we went to hers. It felt strange being there, it felt like an old person's house—it was an old person's house, or had been. There were sheets covering all the pink floral patterned furniture that had obviously been acquired decades ago. It was a big apartment. There was a lot of furniture, a lot of sheets to wash and replace neatly. The caretaker of Carolina's grandmother was still staying there because she was going home to Romania in a couple of days and didn't have anywhere to stay until she left. She kept the place neat—always doing the dishes, the vacuuming, hanging the laundry after the washer was finished—so that it felt like we had a maid, which was a bit awkward but also nice in a way, except that she always bought the cheapest products when she went shopping, no matter what it was, and the way she spoke reminded me of a chimney. And when we first arrived at the apartment, the night we came back, she asked me if we wanted wine and then opened a bottle before I'd answered.

It wasn't my grandmother's place and I'd only been there a few times, so it didn't feel all the same kinds of strange to me as it did to Carolina. She had been close to her grandmother, the only granddaughter, and had even lived in the apartment when she was very young. Her mother and father had just returned from living abroad for a year while her father studied medicine and they hadn't had anywhere to go.

Carolina was sitting in the dark in her old bedroom, the room that her grandmother had died in. I walked down the hallway saying, "Where are you?"

"In here," she said.

When I found her she was sitting all folded up in an armchair, crying towards the window? I put my hand gently on her back and she cried a little bit harder. I closed the door and then went back and sat with Carolina until she got up quickly and said, "I have to get out of this room."

"Okay," I said.

She felt better sitting on the sofa with the soft lights and the calm music coming out of the speakers. Carolina stood up and we danced a little bit on the carpet and then went into the kitchen and made a salad with some things we found in the fridge. The caretaker was in her bedroom with the door shut, watching *Deal or No Deal* on an eleven-inch television screen. I could hear Howie Mandel.

We wandered around the large apartment and looked at the things on the walls and bookshelves. Carolina looked in the closets and drawers but most of the stuff had been taken out and boxed up already—something that her grandmother was in the process of having the Romanian woman do the last time we had been there to visit, the time we promised to come back but never did. I remember Carolina's grandmother motioning around with her arms, saying, "I don't want to leave all this around for everyone to have to deal with. I mean, where did all this stuff come from? Where is it going to go?"

In one of the open boxes, Carolina found a pair of white-framed designer sunglasses with one arm missing. I found the arm and reattached it with a piece of wire from a twisty-tie in the kitchen. She tried them on and looked in the mirror. "Oh darling," she said.

"Let's go to bed," I said.

Carolina slept in the bed, which was small, and I slept on the floor. At first we tried both sleeping in the bed but there wasn't enough space. "Don't you want a mattress?" Carolina asked. "There's one you can take out of the sofa bed in the other room."

"No, that's alright, I'm fine like this," I said. "I like the floor sometimes."

"It's too hard, you can't sleep there," she said.

"No, it's alright. Let me sleep how I want to sleep."

A few minutes later she said, "Are you sure you want to sleep there?"

"Yes," I said.

In the morning Carolina came down onto the floor and got inside the blanket that was covering me. After lying still for a few moments, she kissed my mouth. We didn't have any contraceptives. We used our hands and were quiet. Then we were up and into the bathroom together. Carolina washed her armpits and I peed. I went out and made us coffee and put it on the table in the dining room. Carolina came out and turned the television on and said she wanted tea so I made it for her. I stared at the weatherman and then watched her flick the channel over to music videos, then to something else.

"What are we going to do?" I asked.

"You mean today or forever?" she said.

"Either one, I guess," I said.

"Let's not think about it," she said. I stared at the television screen. A few minutes went by with just the TV making noise. "Do you want to go running?" she said.

"It's raining," I said.

"Do you want to go skiing?" she said. I looked at her and cocked my head.

I said, "Do you want to go to Egypt?" It was kind of funny.

"Do you want to go to the spa?" she said.

"Want to go to the moon?" I said.

"Want to go to—oh, want to go to Iceland?" she said.

"Want to go to the supermarket?" I said.

"Want to go to church?" she said. I laughed at that and then it was silent for a while. We both stared at the television.

"Do you want to go to the outlets?" I said.

"Do you want to go to brunch?" she said.

"Do you want to go to hell?" I said. "Just kidding, yeah, let's go to brunch and then to the outlets."

"What about skiing? We have to make a decision and tell my father, he keeps asking me."

"We can talk about it, just get ready."

"What day is today?"

"I don't know, Friday maybe."

"If it's Friday, I have to decide about the ring," she said. I got Carolina's red book from her bag and handed it to her. She flipped through the pages and found the date. "Yeah, it's Friday. So what should I do? What should we do?"

"I don't know," I said. "I guess we should not do it."

"But then we will have to use condoms and worry more."

"It's okay, I mean, whatever," I said. "We want to see how you feel without the chemicals."

"Yeah, okay," she said. "I won't do it then."

"Okay, then. What are you going to do with the extra ring?"

"Nothing."

"You should sell it on eBay," I said.

"That's probably illegal," she said.

"I was kidding, but anyway you could do that trick people do, like when they want to sell tickets to a sporting event or a concert or something. They just sell a pair of socks for seven hundred dollars and say that the socks come with 'complimentary tickets to the Super Bowl' or something like that."

"Yeah," she said.

We didn't know exactly where we were going to go for brunch when we started driving. We had to decide on the road, which was usually a bad idea because I had to drive which meant that I had to make the car go in certain directions which meant I had to choose those directions so I pressured Carolina into making decisions and she usually said something like, Why do I have to decide where to go? And then I said something like, Because you care more than I do. If I choose some place, you will just say that you don't want to go there. So tell me where you do want to go. And then she'd get a little mad and say, I don't do that. Then I'd say, Okay, let's go to Alternative Economy, and she would say, We always go there. And I'd say, See? And she'd say, Fine, let's go there. Then I'd say, No, no, we'll go somewhere different. And then we would end up going to Alternative Economy because I had to make the car go somewhere and she was being quiet and I couldn't think of anywhere else that had tasty vegetarian options and an ethical business model.

Once we got there, everything was fine. It wasn't crowded and the brunch menu looked good so we sat down at a table near the window in a little section that we had all to ourselves. We chose the vegetarian option from the menu and I poured water from the pitcher into our glasses. While we ate lunch we talked about how terrible the army is, what it does to people. I don't know why we were talking about that. I had a friend who was in special forces training, I was saying, who told me that they put them all in a room and gave them only water to drink and nothing to eat and said that they couldn't come out until every last one of them had pissed themselves.

By the time dessert came, we were too full and had eaten too much already so I opened my napkin and started putting the little pastries inside and wrapping it up. The waiter walked by as I was doing it, so I picked up one of the pastries and took a bite. I watched him clearing off the table behind ours by the window. I thought he was going to drop something but he didn't. He went away and I put the rest of the cookie back in the napkin and put the whole thing in my jacket pocket.

After we paid, and while walking out to the car, we talked about the future, kind of. Carolina said, "We have to decide what to do. I mean, we have to devote some time to thinking about it."

"I don't know," I said.

"I don't mean right now," she said, "but at some point during the day. We should include time for thinking in our days, is what I'm trying to say."

"Okay," I said, "we can do that." My arm was around her waist.

"We are spending the money and I'm worried that it will be gone and then we will want to buy a house somewhere or something and we'll have wasted all the money."

"It won't be a waste, we are being alive, we are doing what we're doing. We'll figure something out. We'll make some money. We'll do something. We won't use it all. Something will happen. Things will be okay, we just have to take it slow."

"Okay," she said. We stopped walking to kiss. When we started walking again, I put myself on the outside of the sidewalk, near the curb, arm around Carolina. Before too long, we got to the car and I opened her door and then closed it after she got inside. I got in, turned the car on and put us on the highway going south. We got off at an exit made just for the outlet center. It was a big place with lots of asphalt for parking and fake old cobblestone streets for walking on. Then there were the stores, from which we got a few things we needed: new pants, a fleece, cheap tee shirts, and a glass of orange juice. While Carolina was trying on pants she also tried on dresses. She was an average sized woman—which happened to be just about my size as well. We could even trade pants.

At home Carolina was on the computer and I watched a television show about the woolly mammoth, learning that it went extinct from over-aggressive hunting by humans. I thought about if it were still around, where it could live. Siberia maybe, probably.

We made love before going to sleep. It was soft and sweet but at one point Carolina did say, "Oh yes, deeper," which I thought was kind of funny but I didn't laugh.

Over the next few weeks Carolina went slowly into a depression that was probably caused by a change in her levels of testosterone and estrogen. That's what we told each other anyway. She had been on birth control for almost two years and was just now stopping, so her body was all messed up. Her energy level was low and everything made her cry, even small things like arriving too late to a movie we wanted to see.

I walked around thinking our relationship would probably end. We didn't talk about it. We didn't talk much about anything. We barely touched each other. We had stopped having sex now. Carolina wasn't interested at all. She wasn't interested in anything except the possibility of chocolate.

Then about a week before Christmas, one Saturday, Carolina told me that it was over and that I should go home, even though she knew I didn't have any other home. I guess she figured that meant my parents' place. I didn't say anything, just sat on the couch staring out at space in front of me. She said, "It's obvious that I'm never going to have sex with you again. Are you happy with that? Are you happy with masturbating in my dead grandma's bathroom?"

I didn't say anything, I didn't even look at her. She said, "Aren't you going to say something?" I didn't say anything. She puffed, said, "I'm going out. By myself." Then she got dressed and ready to go outside. Before she left she said, "You don't think I mean it, but I do," and then slammed the door. I went to the window and watched her walk down the sidewalk. I didn't know what to do, so I walked around the apartment in circles for a while, then went on the Internet and looked at flights and buses to Pennsylvania.

When Carolina came back she was still very angry. She called her mother and yelled at her for messing up her childhood. I sat quietly on the floor in another room rocking myself slightly back and forth. Afterward I made dinner and we ate it and went to bed. Carolina took her pillow and went into another room to sleep and I followed her. I said, "Please, just come to bed like usual."

"Why?" she asked.

"Just, please, this is disturbing," I said.

She didn't say anything and then I said, "I won't be able to sleep. I'll just stare at the ceiling and go crazy."

"Then we'll be in the same boat," she said.

I stayed looking at her for a few seconds and then she said, "Alright," and came back to bed. We fell asleep nowhere near each other.

In the morning I made tea and she wanted to go running so we did. She felt a little better and I told her that I was going to go home for Christmas, that I was looking at flights and that my father would buy the ticket for me. "You asked him already?" she asked.

"No, I didn't say anything about anything yet."

She didn't want to talk about whether or not I should go home. I tried more than once to find out her opinion and she just shrugged her shoulders every time. I told her I didn't want to abandon her but that it felt like she wanted me to go away. She said she didn't want me to go away and that she was sorry. I stayed around. That night we kissed and touched a little in bed which ended up with me running down the street at one in the morning to get condoms from the machine. It was raining out and when I came back she said she couldn't and that she was sorry, that she didn't know what was wrong with her. We fell asleep in our normal spots.

About a week later, just before Christmas, her period had been over for a few days and her natural chemicals were coming back. She was feeling better and on Christmas afternoon pulled me down onto the bed and said, "Let me see it."

I said, "You know where it is."

She was lying on her back and I was straddling her with my knees just below her shoulders. She unbuckled my pants and touched me and kissed me and then put my penis in her mouth. After a little while she told me to put a condom on and then I was inside her.

When it was over we lay together and then did it again, with her on top this time after a short while of being on her stomach.

After we cleaned up, we went to Carolina's mother's house and had a big dinner while watching music video hits from the eighties. After dinner, Carolina's mother was in the kitchen loading the dishwasher and her brother was having a smoke on the balcony. Carolina and I sat on the sofa and watched Sinead O'Connor sing "Nothing Compares 2 U."

On the way out to the car, going home, Carolina tripped on a tree root and landed hard on her knee, scraping her hand. At home we cleaned up the wound and watched a movie and went to bed.

Carolina's father was in the house when I woke up the next morning. I heard his voice, put my jeans on and then walked out of the bedroom pushing my head through the hole in my t-shirt. They were in the dining room talking about tire chains. I heard him say, "I will buy the chains for the car today and bring it back over tomorrow morning." I walked into the dining room. The way he was sitting in the chair, he looked like an English professor driving a big rig.

"Oh, we're taking the car?" I said.

"Yeah," Carolina said, "it's better."

"Yeah, it's fine, I just didn't know it was decided that we were even going."

"Yeah, we were talking about it," she said.

"Yeah it's good, okay. Good, when do we leave?"

"I think you ought to leave on the fifth," her father said. "We're going to be up there from the first to the fifth, if you come on the fifth we can leave the gas and water on, it will be better."

"You aren't taking the car?" I said.

"No, we're going by train," he said.

"Yeah, but don't you usually take the car on the train?" I said.

"We're renting a car this time. It's easier."

"Okay, sounds good," I said walking into the kitchen. "Where's the coffee?" I said.

After breakfast Carolina was watching *Gremlins 2* on television and I asked her if she wanted to go ice skating or biking or if she wanted to bike to the ice skating rink or somewhere else or something else, anything. She was nodding her head at me and saying yes but watching these little gremlins moving around. One of them got stuffed into the garbage disposal and there was blood everywhere. I said "gross" and she laughed and turned the television off and looked at me.

"What's wrong?" I said. "You don't feel well?"

"I'm tired of my father supporting me. I want to tell him to stop giving me money, giving us money," she said.

I didn't say anything.

"What have we been doing here since we got back? We are just wasting our time and money."

"It's the holidays," I said. "We are relaxing, getting mental rest."

"When aren't we relaxing or getting mental rest?" she said.

I didn't say anything. I was sitting in a rocking chair in the middle of the room. She was at the table.

"I feel like I am six years old. I don't want to feel that way anymore. I don't want my father to support me anymore. I am such a joke. I am not a person. What am I? What have I ever done that was worth anything? What have I ever even done? I just start all kinds of projects and never finish any of them. Why didn't I graduate? Why do I have a guitar I never play? I don't even know what I'm doing."

I didn't say anything. I rocked gently back and forth in the chair. Carolina went into the bedroom and lay on the bed. I followed her and sat on the floor looking at her.

"Do you want to be alone?" I said. I thought she said yes but I wasn't sure. I stayed there.

She said, "What do you want?"

"Nothing," I said. I was surprised at her question. I brought my hands up to my head and touched my temples with my fingers. I wondered why I was doing that, if it was because I had seen other people do it in similar situations or if I just didn't know what else to do, but it felt good to touch my forehead. She started to cry and I started bringing my hands towards my head again and then stopped and quickly left the room. I went back to the rocking chair and thought about what I would do if she sent me home. I thought about what I would tell people. I didn't know what to say or think. I thought about writing Carolina an email from home that said, "How are you?" Then I thought that would be stupid.

I went back into the bedroom and said, "Can I sit in here with you?"

She didn't say anything so I stayed. After a few minutes she got up and left the room. I went out after her. I found her in the kitchen eating a banana and when I tried to touch her arm she made a sour face and walked away quickly into another room. I stayed in the kitchen for a few minutes and then went into the hallway near the front door and sat down. I stayed there for a while thinking about what I would say to people at home. I thought about telling them that Carolina was severely depressed and needed to get herself out of it, to create stability for herself, that I couldn't be around, that I would make things worse, that it was only for a little while. I was working it out in my head, how to say it, how to space it out, which things to say first, which things not to say at all. I would explain that by being around I was giving her excuses, giving her something to lean on. I would use familiar phrases and idioms so that I wouldn't have to think about what I was saying. I would reiterate that she needed to create stability for herself. That would be a very important thing I would say to people. I thought it sounded pretty good. I thought that I might be able to get by for a while on all that, but I didn't know what I would do. And I didn't have any money. I'd have to ask Carolina for money to get to the airport, I thought. I heard her speak from the other room. She said, "Don't you wish you never met me?"

"Do you wish you never met me?" I said walking into the bedroom.

"Do you wish you never met me?" she said again.

"No," I said.

"I'm so stupid. I have problems," she said.

I didn't say anything. I sat on the floor by the hallway.

"I am like a stupid girl in mourning for herself. I should just kill myself. I'm really going to kill myself," she said.

I didn't say anything.

"I just have to think about how I'll do it," she said.

She had talked about it before. She had done this whole kind of show before, too. I knew she wouldn't do it, but for some reason I felt like it was more serious this time, more desperate.

"There is no way out of this. What can I do to get out of this?" she asked.

I didn't say anything. I said almost nothing the whole time.

"Well?" she said, "what do you say about it, what can we do?"

"I don't know," I said.

"Great," she said. "A lot of use you are."

"Are you angry at me?" I said.

"Yes," she said.

"Why?" I said.

"I don't know. Because you're stupid too. We're both just stupid people who don't know how to be alive. We shouldn't be together." Then she said, "Actually, we deserve each other. Who else would be with either of us? We're so weak and, and, and, and we're just children," she said. "We're children."

She cried again. I waited there, sitting. She stopped crying and we stayed there a long time, not looking at each other or speaking. I thought about how many times we've been through this and wondered how many more times we would get into it. I got up and went out to the living room and sat on the couch. She came out and sat on a chair near the couch. The chair still had a sheet covering it. The phone rang and Carolina stopped crying to answer it. It was her father about the tire chains and to find out what shoe size I was because he found an extra pair of old snow boots lying around and thought I might be able to use them. She didn't say much besides yes and okay and that I was a size nine or so. Then she hung up. We talked more and Carolina said that she had to give up on trying to be some kind of artist or bullshit person who felt the need to prove herself. She cried and let me touch her. I laid my head in her lap while I wrapped my arms around behind her knees. I was sitting, sort of squatting, on the floor near the chair she was in. After a while I said, "I want to figure things out with you. We'll figure things out."

She felt better and sat on the couch with her head in my lap. We talked about how it was when we first met, a little about the sex but mostly about cooking dinner. Then Carolina felt hungry so we started dinner. We made baked potatoes cut open and stuffed with broccoli and corn with a little curry yogurt sauce.

After dinner we watched *Deal or No Deal* on television and I read *Calvin & Hobbes* out loud in bed before turning out the light. After the light was out we were thinking about our childhoods and Carolina asked me if I ever loved a girl who didn't love me back.

I said, "Well, what do you mean by loved? If you mean like a crush, then yeah, I have."

"Yeah, that," she said. "Who was she?"

"This girl in high school. She was older than me. I was probably sixteen. She would have been seventeen I guess."

"What did you do?"

"Nothing," I said.

"What do you mean, nothing?"

"I don't know, what do you mean?"

"I mean, did you tell her or try to kiss her or what?"

"No, I mean we were kind of friends. She knew I liked her."

"So you didn't touch her."

"No, I don't know. It was weird."

We were on our sides, my back facing her, her rubbing it. "Scratch," I said.

She scratched my back and said, "Oh, yes, I love this part, dead skin cells underneath my fingernails, just piling up."

"Sorry," I said.

"No, no," she said.

She scratched my back for a little longer and then I rolled over onto it and lay looking at the light coming through the blinds and landing on the ceiling. I could almost slow it down looking at it for a long time, so that it was like someone outside was constantly turning a light on and I could see it moving through the air. There was never darkness except in the spots where the slats blocked the light off at an angle. I thought about how a black woman would look naked. I thought about the light flesh color of her vagina contrasted against the dark skin of her thighs and black pubic hair. "I think Mary Poppins is great," Carolina said.

"What?" I said.

"Really, she's great. I think I want to be Mary Poppins."

I laughed.

"I've never thought about actually being Mary Poppins before. It's such a great thought," she said.

"Okay, you can be Mary Poppins tomorrow," I said.

"Okay, yes," she said.

What we'd been doing all this time was waiting for something to happen. At least, that's what I was thinking we'd been doing. I wondered how long it would go on.

We hadn't talked about it except in an indirect way. We said that maybe what we needed was a simple life, a peaceful one, something we felt we could sustain. We didn't really believe it was going to happen, I don't think. By this point, neither of us had much faith in our ability to plan something and then execute that plan. We weren't action people, we were reaction people. We were erratic and unreliable—moody, I guess, is what most others would call it. Toward the end of winter in her grandma's apartment, I felt more like a building than a person. Like one of those nuclear reactors, except a nuclear reactor knew what it should be doing.

We loved each other even when we weren't in love. We chose to love each other. There wasn't much else that we chose to do—eat dinner, watch movies—but both of us could tell that it wasn't going to be enough, and there were so many times in a day when we could choose to go the other way. And maybe we did for a short while before giving up on that way too, then resolved everything with hugs on the bed, which we loved easily because the bed was an easy place to be.

When we were on the bed, in those times, we didn't really hug, we just lay together with my chest on top and hers on the bottom. Her legs would be open and mine would be between them so that it was like when we were making love the sweet way but we weren't and we had our clothes on and we let our weight push against each other sometimes and sometimes go the same way and it was like we had one same force and our energies matched up perfectly. It was better than building a hug machine, we decided one day lying together. I'd said, "Do you wish we had a hug machine?" and she'd said, "No," and that it was better our way—that our way was better, and that it was ours.

The holidays passed—Christmas and then New Year's. On the fifth, Carolina and I took her father's car and drove up to his place in the mountains, just like they had all planned out. We woke up early to start driving. It was about a nine hour drive up to the place in Vermont, not far from the Canadian border. When we arrived it was late and I'd done all the driving. We couldn't find our building in the dark. Carolina didn't remember the place well enough and I'd never been there. She called her father to ask how to find it but he wasn't answering and it was a bit icy and I was out of the car slipping on the ice trying to read a street sign. A lady walked by asking if we needed help and I said we didn't, but she persisted. She was a small, elderly woman. Eventually she sent us on our way to the place—it was right up the road but we had given up too soon. The car had little traction on the curvy mountain road, which was icy, so we parked halfway down at the leisure center and walked the rest of the way up. I made three trips to get all our bags. The box with the food and kitchen stuff was the heaviest, and for some reason I'd left it until last. I struggled up the road. With city shoes on I had to stop more than a few times, but eventually I made it and, exhausted, I spread myself out on the bed. Carolina had the television on, flipping through, trying to find something to watch. I told her to stop on a nature show and she did and said, "I knew you'd say that," and I looked up at the ceiling and then used a pillow to support my head so I could see foxes ripping apart a little rodent. "Oh, no," Carolina said. "No, how cruel."

"The circle of life or whatever," I said.

"It's cruel," she said.

"Life is cruel, making me carry heavy boxes up icy hills."

"No, I'm the cruel one," she said.

"It's okay, I am the big strong man, I do the man's work."

"What are we going to do tomorrow and for the rest of the time?" she said.

"Well, the worst part is over, we got all the stuff up, if we have to leave the car there and walk to and from it, it's not the worst thing ever. I just hope it doesn't snow much more."

That next day we were out getting groceries and toilet paper and stuff like that and it started to snow while we were in the supermarket. It started slow and then came quicker and started spreading itself out on the street and I was worried so I hurried Carolina along, which she wasn't too happy about, but we made it back up to the pool parking lot and walked the rest of the way up again. At the top, in the room, Carolina was unhappy about the prospect of walking up and down all the time, so she called her father and talked to him about the ice and he told her to go down to the garage in the morning and have them put snow tires on and that he would pay for them, so that's what we did. After the tires were on, driving around was easy and we could go up and down and all kinds of other ways too without any problem.

When we'd picked up the car from the garage after ice skating at the town rink, there were all four old tires sitting in the back in big plastic bags. I backed the car out of the tire room and when Carolina got inside near the street I said, "Guess what."

She said, "What?" in a little bit of worry and I said, "They put the old tires in the back."

"Oh," she said, "the way you said it, I thought something was wrong."

She called her father and asked him what to do and he said we should pick the two best tires to keep and throw the others away. When Carolina told me what he said, I laughed. I said, "How do I know what tires are better, and where are we supposed to dump the others, in the river?"

"Yeah, I don't know," she said.

"He can sort it out when we get home," I said.

While we were ice skating I heard a couple of guys with Canadian accents. I skated by, mentioning it to Carolina who said, "What?" and then I skated by again saying it again and she said, "What?" again so the next time I stopped and said it slowly in the manner that people speak to children and dogs. She responded by making a face that was like, oh, that's all? and then made a movement with her head and said, "Go make some friends." I skated over to the guys where they stopped to rest on the side and I asked them where they were from and what they were doing down here and I told them that we had come up for a little mountain get-away or something like that. When I skated back to Carolina I told her they were from Saskatchewan. She laughed and said, "I didn't mean them, I meant those guys over there." She was pointing at a guy/girl couple skating around shakily.

"What?" I said.

"Yeah, I meant them, didn't you hear them?"

"No," I said.

"They have southern accents," she said.

"I was talking about the Canadian guys," I said.

"What Canadian guys?"

"I'm so confused," I said.

"Go talk to those people," Carolina said, pointing with her chin.

"No, I'm done talking to people I don't know," I said. "Today I talked to enough people I don't know to last me the rest of the year."

"But we just started a new year," Carolina said.

"That I know," I said.

"Whatever, shut up."

"Yes, ma'am," I said skating away backwards.

When we were tired of skating we went inside to change back into our shoes. We sat on benches and watched the couple from out the window. Carolina said, "Do you wish we had friends?"

"Sometimes," I said.

"We are funny," she said.

"Yeah," I said.

Later, driving back to our room, Carolina was grouchy.

"Somebody needs a beer," I said.

"I'm going to take a bath."

"You totally stole my idea," I said.

"It doesn't matter, I said it out loud first," she said.

"We can take a bath together," I said.

"It's too small for that."

"Okay then I can take a bath while you do yoga and you can come and be in the bathtub for like a few minutes with me and then I will get out and you can have a bath by yourself in comfort."

"I don't want to bathe in your old bath water," she said.

"Isn't there a song about that?" I said, "Except I think it says the opposite, that someone does want to bathe in someone else's old bath water."

"I don't know," she said, "I was just kidding anyway, I'd love to wash in your old bath water."

"That's it," I said, "that's how it goes." She gave me a look like, duh.

From in the bathroom while the water was filling up the tub, I heard Carolina say something. I went out into the room. She was arched with her feet and hands down at different ends of the yoga mat, her posterior up in the air.

"Sarah Jessica Parker is single again," she said. I laughed.

"That's it?" I said.

"What?"

"That's what you said?"

I walked back into the bathroom and closed the door, which I reopened right away to say something but I looked at her and nothing came out of my mouth. She was moving into another position with her legs stretched almost parallel with the floor up to her hands which rested palms flat on the ground. The trunk of her body proceeded upwards with the head tilted back, eyes looking at whatever's on the ceiling. Upward Facing Dog.

Fifteen minutes later, when she came into the bathroom, my head was under the water and my eyes were closed so I didn't see her. I felt her hand take hold of my penis and I opened my eyes. She was kneeling and bent over the tub. I arched my back and brought my pelvis out of the water and she kissed it. When she got into the tub, I said, "Better be careful, little sperm can survive in warm water."

"They could never swim this distance," she said, "it takes them like two days to swim an inch in the uterus."

"Yeah but they are fighting hazardous conditions in there," I said.

After a little while I got out of the tub but first I pulled the plug to drain some water and then turned on the faucet to add new water.

"I was kidding about the dirty bath water thing," she said.

"No, I know," I said, "but it's still better to have some fresh water."

"Thank you," she said, chirpily, like a little bird.

After that, I left the bathroom and went out into the living room and to the sliding glass door to look out and down on the little town with all the little orange lights.

Later Carolina came out of the bath. We made dinner, ate it, watched a zombie movie that her brother had put on the hard drive for us, and then went to bed. Before sleeping we had sex and before entering her, on top, arms outstretched holding myself up in the air, I didn't want to put a condom on but I did and afterward we slept, bodies close to each other under the fleece blanket.

I watched Carolina from the balcony as she took the road that wound down the hill from our building. She slipped on ice and fell, but not too hard. I waved on the chance that she was looking up, but she wasn't and I knew it and I watched her all the rest of the way down and in through the automatic sliding doors of the leisure center. I had been drinking a Belgian-style tripel in a fat wine glass with a short stem and when I saw Carolina step through the sliding doors, I thought about throwing the glass from my hand through the air towards the roof across the way from me and a little down the hill, but I didn't. I went back inside and closed our own sliding glass door. Then I put the glass down on the table and sat on the bed with my left leg tucked under me.

After a while sitting alone in a chair replaying the previous day in my mind, I stopped remembering, got my body up and moving, and turned on a light. I tried to read a book but I couldn't concentrate so I ate some cheese from the refrigerator and thought about what we could make for dinner later. I walked over to look out the sliding glass door and decided that I would go pick Carolina up with the car. It was only a half a minute drive down to the leisure center, but I knew she would appreciate not having to walk back up, especially after being loosened and relaxed by the sauna, hammam, jacuzzi, swimming, or whatever else.

I looked for her in the dark on the road on the way down just in case she was already out and walking up but I didn't see her. I thought about the possibility of her having taken the dirt trail that cuts up steeper but I knew she wouldn't have done that because I suggested the idea a few times the day before and she was always against it. One of the times, I had forced her to do it anyway and she didn't like it at all and I agreed that it was a bit too slippery and probably a stupid thing to do, but we didn't turn back.

I waited in the lobby of the leisure center, near the sign that said snack bar but was just a few vending machines. I didn't see her there by the locker room exit where the hairdryers were but I figured she would be out soon because she'd been down there for a long time, so I waited sitting on a radiator reading and rereading the preface to the first collection of Hemingway short stories published by Charles Scribner's Sons in 1938. I was always reading those stories.

Carolina came out of the locker room, dried her hair with a hairdryer attached by a chord to the wall and then walked up the steps into the lobby. She didn't see me at first so I walked towards where she was walking towards and then she saw me. She smiled and said, "Were you trying to get in?"

"No, I just came to pick you up," I said.

"On foot or with the car?"

"With the car," I said. "I thought you might like to not have to walk up."

"Yes, that is great, thank you, my sweet boy."

"No, I am a man, a big strong man."

"Oh, right, yes," she said with a deeper voice. "Thank you my big strong man."

"Why do you have the deep voice? I am the man."

"Oh, right, sorry," she said and laughed.

"This-a-way, darling," I said pushing open the door and holding it for her to walk through first. I followed her out and we took the car up to the parking lot of our building and then the elevator to our floor. The room was warm and stale when we got inside so I opened the sliding door to let some new air in.

On a snowy morning we took the computer down to a café on the corner that had wireless Internet. I drove us down and we parked close to the place, on the street, paid the meter and then walked up the outdoor steps to the second floor and then inside the cafe. I ordered a *café Viennois* and Carolina ordered chocolate *Viennois*. *Viennois* is a French kind of drink where they put whipped cream on the top of everything. Being close to the border of Quebec, there was a lot of typical French stuff around at the restaurants and all. One night when we'd been out eating dinner Carolina saw snails on the menu and pointed it out to me. In a slow southerly voice I'd said, "Snails … he had those in his pockets, too," and she'd laughed.

We ordered our drinks standing right inside the door before we sat down. The owners were pleasant and nice. We looked around and chose a table but then I changed my mind and we went to another one. The sun was coming in through the window even with the snow. It looked strange. The flakes were large and soft and you could see the crystals on them. They fell slowly and you could watch them for a long time, which I did while Carolina was in the bathroom.

I took the computer out of my backpack to turn it on and Carolina said, "Already? Why don't you wait a little while, it's nice here."

"Okay," I said and set the computer down on top of my pack on the floor between my chair and the window which took up the entire wall from floor to ceiling.

The interior of the cafe was done in a farmhouse style: all knotty pine walls, natural color, and large wooden support beams exposed and running along the ceiling. There were antique iron hand-held farm tools hanging and laying around. I turned my head in every direction looking at them all, and at the quilts on the back wall away from the fireplace.

"Can you go down and get us a paper?" Carolina said.

"Now?" I said.

"Yeah, it would be nice."

"We can read the news online," I said.

"No, but I want to read the actual paper. I want to hold it."

So I went down and came back up a few minutes later with two different newspapers. I put them down on the table where our drinks now were. I took off my coat, sat down, and put sugar in my coffee. I stirred it and took a sip. "Good," I said.

"Do you think I should cut my hair?" Carolina said.

"I don't know. If you want to, yeah."

"I was thinking about cutting it short."

"You should cut it weird like with some strands still very long but the majority much shorter."

"Really?"

"That would be good," I said.

"I don't know."

"You should do it yourself. In the mirror. I will hold another mirror behind you so you can see everything."

"Or you could do it."

"No, it's better to cut your hair yourself."

"What? Why?"

"I don't know. It just is."

"Okay, weirdo."

"Don't call me a weirdo, you're the one with the hair strands that are drastically different lengths."

"Not yet I'm not."

"Okay, fine," I said, "have your boring old normal person's hair. Eat some snails while you're at it."

"Ew, no. And besides, I wanted to cut my hair short a long time ago and you said no, let it grow long and I said don't have boring tastes."

"I remember," I said, "and now it's long."

"Do you want to get something to eat?" she said.

"I don't know, is there soup?" I said.

"I don't want to go home tomorrow," she said.

"Why not?"

"Because it feels nice being here. What are we going to do when we get home?"

"I don't know. Don't think about it now. Just be here in the sun and think about being here. In the sun."

"Okay," she said.

We left late the next morning, just before lunch, but didn't go far. We stopped in a little town, an old town, not even an hour away from where we were. Carolina wanted to get a room and stay there for the night. She had remembered being there in that town when she was younger, with her father, and she'd wanted to see it again.

We didn't want to spend money on dinner so we went to a supermarket and bought fruit, bread, and a quinoa salad from the cold section. We bought the cheapest fork they had—it was a dollar thirty-nine—then walked back to the motel and went upstairs to our room.

I spent almost half an hour trying to get the little price sticker off of the fork. For some reason they'd put it on the metal part, on the part you put in your mouth, and not on the handle. I finally got the sticker off and washed the fork really well a lot of times in the bathroom sink. Before we ate Carolina said, "Did you wash it good?"

"Yes, ma'am" I said.

That night we had sex before watching a movie. In town we'd found a store with used DVDs and bought two independent British films we'd never heard of for four dollars each. After we'd eaten we lay there on the bed, touching and digesting at the same time. We liked having sex in motels because nothing there was ours and we didn't care about the sheets, except for whoever ended up having to sleep on the wet spot but there wouldn't be a wet spot anymore because we were using condoms again.

In the morning we paid for parking and went home. We stopped to see a friend on the way, staying the night so that the drive wasn't all in one day. He took us to a local film club where we watched a movie about an architect from Philadelphia. At one point, back in the sixties, he'd wanted to redesign Center City Philadelphia so that you parked your car outside and walked in. I thought about how great that would have been. The movie got a little boring but we were drinking wine for cheap—red wine—and I started to think about Carolina and her being naked and the sex we'd had the night before. I thought about all the motels we'd had sex in. All of the different kinds of rooms and beds, how they were what changed while the kind of sex we had stayed the same.

In the morning we got coffee and pastries at a place nearby and then went driving home. We stopped in a little Appalachian Trail town somewhere in New York for lunch. I had tomato basil soup with a hummus veggie wrap and Carolina had the soup with a Greek salad.

THREE

I Don't Know

When we got back from the mountains, everything went back to being the way it was before. It was still Carolina's grandmother's apartment, and she was still dead. Carolina asked what we should do and I never had an answer.

She was less angry about it this time. We sat down on couch pillows on the floor in the middle of the living room. We lit Japanese incense and played something like Mahler quietly. We started off by breathing deeply and saying "Ohm" a few times. It was all Carolina's idea. I went along. We got out notepads and pencils and sat there talking about our future. We agreed to write down whatever we thought about, not to filter, to sort it out later. So we mentioned things we'd like to do or things we needed, we took turns. Carolina said, "I have been thinking about writing my thesis finally. I think it would be good to get some closure with that, but I just don't know if I'll be able to do it. Maybe I should just let it go entirely."

"Okay," I said and nodded. Carolina asked me what I wanted and I didn't know what to say. She said, "Come on, don't think about it, just answer."

"Empty time," I said.

"What do you mean?" she said. I shrugged, but she pursued it, so I just started saying stuff without thinking about it, like she wanted.

"Somebody said if you want to get one good hour of painting done, you need four good hours of uninterrupted time," I said.

"You're not a painter," she said.

"I know," I said.

"Well, whatever, okay," she said.

"Well, it's kind of like that anyway," I said.

"Okay," she said, "I'm writing this down."

"Your turn," I said.

"Wait, that's it? Say something else," she said.

"I don't know," I said.

"Okay," she said, "well, talk more about the empty time, I mean, we have a lot of time."

"Yeah, but we spend it worried about what we're going to do with our lives. It's different, I need peaceful time, or, whatever, I don't know. Maybe I don't need anything. What does it matter anyway?" I said.

We sat quietly for a while in thought and then we talked about other things that we wanted to do or things we felt we needed. We talked about traveling more. Carolina talked about something that she'd talked a lot about before: external energy. She talked about needing energy and forces from outside of her and us to be present and positive effects on us.

She said, "This is something I've always needed my whole life. When I met you, you were it—a very good positive force coming from outside myself—but now you are inside. So it doesn't work the same way anymore."

"You want a new man," I said.

"No, no, no, no, no, no, that's not it at all," she said.

"I know," I said. "I was just kidding. I understand what you are saying."

The phone rang and ended our brainstorming session. Carolina went off into another room talking and I lay on the hard floor with my head turned looking out the window. It was mid-afternoon and lightly raining and all I could really see from my angle was the streetlamp that made the electricity sound I heard at night when it was on. I saw it coming out above the tops of little trees that had grown up from the street. I thought about the tree roots spread out below the surface of the asphalt and looked at the metal casing of the streetlamp, which, besides the rust that had collected there, matched up perfectly with the color of the sky so that it seemed to disappear. On other days I'd seen the lamp set against blue sky. At night, when it was on and humming, and especially if it was a foggy night, the glow at that angle setting it off into space made it seem like a really close star. I stayed there on the floor for a while with the sound of car tires making rain splash off in the distance somewhere not too far away and I wondered why the sound was as loud as it was. Then it was quieter and I noticed the plants outside on the balcony, drooping and thirsty, so I got up to give them water. The balcony door was locked but I found the key and a watering can. Carolina had come in the room while I was out there and hadn't noticed me, but I saw her through the window moving around the room. She moved gracefully. She had let down her long brown hair, which was split by her shoulder blades. She was naked except for a pair of tight blue underwear and thinly striped socks that went halfway up her calves. When she turned to leave the room I saw her breasts for a moment and then she was gone. I went back inside and laid myself down in the same spot on the floor where I was before and I stared out the window without doing much looking. I was thinking about Carolina and about her hair and about how I'd been thinking that I wanted her to cut it but that it looked so nice just then. I thought about her hair outside down in the wind going around our faces and I thought about it coming down past my head, soft on my ears when she was on top in the middle of the afternoon some afternoon.

Carolina re-entered the room, speaking as she came through the doorway. "Were you there the whole time?"

"What whole time?" I said, knowing what she meant.

"Nothing, never mind. Never you mind," she said and took a few steps, then turned back. "I mean, I came in the room before and I swear you weren't there."

"I've been here looking out the window," I said.

"Weird," she said. "I mean, I'd have had to step over you." Then she thought about it and said, "You couldn't have been there."

"I was here," I said.

She looked at me, confused, and said, "It's impossible." I shrugged my shoulders. She was wearing pants now, jeans, with a brown belt, and a bra but still no shirt, which was in her hand, hanging down, one sleeve touching the floor just near my head.

"It's raining," I said.

"Is it?" she said.

"Yeah, I was out there. I watered the plants," I said. I was pointing.

"Oh good, I've been meaning to say we needed to do that but I kept forgetting," she said. Then, "Wait, when were you out there?"

"Just before, a few minutes ago when you came in the room half naked," I said, then she swung down and smacked me on the arm.

"What?" I asked, smiling.

"You're. Not. Funny," she said, hitting me on the beat of her words. "You made me think I was crazy," she said, "how could you say that and be so convincing?"

"I'll teach you someday," I said and laughed.

"Anyway, it's time for yoga class, can you drive me?"

"Yes," I said.

I put my shoes and coat on and grabbed the umbrella near the front door as we went out of it, closing it behind us. I locked the door and Carolina called the elevator and we took it down to the basement where the car was parked.

I dropped Carolina off in front of the building where her yoga class was and we said we'd meet there again at three fifteen. I found a parking spot and walked to get a piece of pizza for lunch. It had stopped raining but started again lightly while I was walking around in the streets after eating so I ran to the car without thinking and got in one of the back doors. I sat there and it rained harder—so hard that I couldn't think. I liked the sound of it but it didn't last very long and I was out again and walking around and watching my own footsteps.

I met Carolina to pick her up from yoga class and we went to get ice cream. After we ate ice cream I said that we still had time left on the parking meter so we walked along a commercial street and looked at shops and went into some of them. Carolina tried some clothes on, just for fun, and then we saw her brother riding his bicycle in the street. We called out to him and he stopped and we talked for a few minutes. Then he went on his way and we went on ours— back towards the car, stopping to buy Carolina some new socks because all of hers were starting to get holes in them.

I still had no idea what we were going to do.

The next day, Carolina spent all afternoon, from one to five, locked in the spare bedroom with the door closed and the computer on. I wandered around the apartment not knowing what to do and then sat on the couch and read Hemingway which made me want to move to Key West or Ketchum, Idaho or a ranch near Cooke City, Montana. It was sunny outside and I thought about taking a walk but I didn't. I thought about all of the people and places I'd wanted to be and go to. I thought about the places Carolina and I had gone, about the plans we had and did and the plans we had and didn't do. I thought about the plans we didn't have now and wondered what would happen to us in the future which seemed to be getting closer and closer and I thought about how most of the time I tried not to think about it.

I thought about what I'd do if we broke up, about where I'd go. There were a million places I could think of going, and it felt good to think about them lying there in the sunlight which was a little too warm until I reached up and slid the window open. Cool air came over me and it felt nice and fresh and I breathed it in and thought, "I'm going to remember this air, breathing it in," and I did remember it.

Sometime after lunch, late, when the sun had gone down but it wasn't completely dark yet, I told Carolina I was going for a walk and asked if she wanted to come. She said, "Where is there to walk? We've been everywhere."

"I don't know," I said. "Maybe we haven't been everywhere. Maybe there is a nice little street somewhere, quiet, with a slight breeze, or maybe there isn't and there are cars and dog stuff all over the ground, or maybe there's a surf shop or, you know, whatever."

"There's not a surf shop, we are hours from the ocean," she said.

"Do you want to come along or what?"

"Okay."

"Okay, but you have to be nice and just go where I am going. Let's just pretend that you are invisible and I am going on a walk and you get to watch what it's like," I said.

"Okay," she said.

We left the apartment and went out starting up the street. Carolina said, "We're going this way?" And I just looked at her. She said, "Sorry," and laughed.

We walked down some boring streets that we'd been down a thousand times and then up past the Library Bus, which is this little library on wheels that goes around to different parts of the city where there isn't a library close by so that people can go and pick up books that they ordered or just look around and maybe sign something out. I asked Carolina if she wanted to go inside but she said no and then I insisted, saying that I wanted to see the inside of the Library Bus, that I never had before. She said, "What good is the inside of a Library Bus if you aren't going there to get something?"

"I just want to see what it's like inside. Have you ever seen the inside of a Library Bus?" I asked.

"No," she said.

"Aren't you curious?" I said. "Maybe it will alter your worldview. Do you want your worldview altered?"

She didn't say anything. She was trying to see inside the back window of the bus which was pretty high up off the ground.

"See, you do want to see it, but you're just afraid of the Library Bus Guy," I said.

"Who is the Library Bus Guy?" she said.

"I don't know and neither do you and that's why you're afraid of him," I said and laughed.

"Shut up, I am not afraid of the Library Bus Guy," Carolina said.

"Okay, whatever you say," I said.

We walked down and around the curve. It was getting darker out and we came to a little opening between the buildings and a field with grass that had grown up pretty high so that it was hard to walk through. It had rained the day before so the ground was soft and muddy in spots. When we came into the clearing Carolina said, "Hey, I've never seen this before."

And I said, "Yeah, it's nice."

"It would be nice to live there," Carolina said, pointing at a corner apartment at the top of a building towards the furthest edge of the field. "Peaceful."

On the way back towards home we saw a small little street and Carolina said, "Hey, what's this?" And I said, "I don't know, let's check it out." We walked along it and came to a bad looking tattoo shop, dirty, with a terrible storefront sign. When I saw it I said, "Yes, that's what I want to see when I'm walking into a place where they put ink on my body forever." Then I said, "Let's see what's further."

"There's another shop," Carolina said. When we got close enough she said, "No. No way. You totally knew this was here. What is this doing here?"

I laughed and pretended I knew and that this was all by design, but I'd never been there before.

"The lady inside looks so bored. Let's go in?"

"Okay," I said.

It was some kind of junk shop-gypsy-fortune-teller type of place. I was positive it hadn't been there even a couple of weeks ago, but it seemed like a place that had been around forever. We were the only ones in the store and when we walked in, the lady smiled at us and said hello but then left us alone for a while as we walked around and looked at stuff. That was nice of her. She was short and round with black hair down below her chin, all cut at exactly the same length but stringy, and she spoke with what sounded like a German accent. When we finally got around to talking to her we found out she was Belgian and that her shop had been there for thirteen years. That seemed like a convenient number for a fortuneteller psychic lady and I didn't believe her one bit. She said she liked us and wanted to read our palms free of charge. "On the house," is how she said it. Carolina really wanted to do it and I said I would just watch but she protested, so I said I'd do it too. The psychic lady didn't really say much of anything about Carolina. She said, "You have great highs and great lows in life," and then suggested a tarot reading would better suit her so they did that. I had no idea about Tarot so I kind of zoned out for a while but apparently the tower card came out in reference to personal relationships in Carolina's life. I had no idea what that meant but I came to understand that it was a very terrible thing. Apparently it represents war and means that everything could come crashing down soon. I understood it to be sort of like the parable about what will happen if you build your house on a foundation of sand. That's what came to my mind when she was explaining it. Carolina was kind of freaked out which got me out of having to get my palm read because she just wanted to leave. While we were trying to get out of there gracefully, the psychic lady asked if we wanted to participate in a free massage session. I didn't quite understand the idea, but supposedly it was a massage where no parts of the body are untouched and "anything that happens in the normal course of things is okay." We pretended to seem interested and told her that we had to go but maybe would do it another time.

We went back out to a busier street and decided to stop at a bakery and eat some little pastries, which we did out on a table under an awning just across the sidewalk.

"That lady was … nice," I said.

Carolina laughed but didn't seem to want to talk about it. I thought maybe the tarot reading was still bothering her. I didn't push it. We just ate our snacks and then headed for home. There were two routes and we took the longer one. At some point I said, "Sometimes I think we should just live in a city and have part time jobs."

"Yeah," Carolina said, "but a nice part time job, like at a cafe that has good art books and is never too busy but busy enough."

"Yeah or at a bookstore, or a library," I said.

"You could be Library Bus Guy," Carolina said.

"Yes," I said and laughed. "That would be awesome."

On the way home we passed the Library Bus again and Library Bus Guy was standing at the little back window, hanging out, smoking a cigarette with a mean face on. To Carolina I said, "You can't be Library Bus Guy and lean out the window smoking and have a bad face on. It's like, 'Hey kids, don't read books, smoke cigarettes instead and have terribly unwelcoming facial expressions.'"

Carolina laughed and said, "You would make a way better Library Bus Guy."

"I so would," I said.

At home we listened to music and Carolina worked on her photographs while I read Hemingway, sometimes thinking about what he must have looked like when he was twenty-six, trying to picture it in my head.

I t's incredible to me that people make houses and roads and buildings," Carolina said. "I don't understand it."

I didn't say anything. I wanted to laugh but I didn't.

"How can anyone care enough?" Carolina said.

"That I don't know," I said. "That is a mystery to me, too."

"What are we going to do?" Carolina said.

"I don't know," I said.

There was silence. I looked at Carolina but she didn't look at me. She stared ahead into space and I thought she was thinking about how I never have anything to say except "I don't know."

"Let's go to Mexico," I said.

"What?"

"Let's go to Mexico."

"To live?"

"No, I don't know. To nothing. We'll just go and see. We'll see Mexico and we'll see. We can go to my parents and get my old car. My dad will make sure it is all tuned up and ready to go and we'll drive to Mexico. We'll go down through Georgia, Mississippi, Louisiana, Texas. We can go to Florida first if you want. We can go to the Keys. We can see Hemingway's old house. We can see his cats, or the offspring of his cats."

"The offspring of his cats are there?" Carolina said.

"Must be," I said.

"Is that cool?" she said.

"I don't know," I said.

"What about money?"

"What do you mean?"

"Going to Mexico costs money."

"We'll, um, we could take our clothes off for money."

"Shut up."

"People would pay to watch us have sex."

"Stop being stupid. I'm being serious."

"Well, we're here now and we're spending money on being alive and we don't have jobs and we're not working and we would spend less money to be alive in Mexico because it's much cheaper, so if we stay there for a while then the difference in cost of living would eventually cover the cost of gas to get there," I said.

"I don't think that's true."

"Yeah, I don't know."

"How long can we be in Mexico?"

"What do you mean, like, how long are we allowed to be there?"

"Yeah."

"Three months probably. We can look it up. But I think it's easy to get permission to stay longer."

Carolina sat down on the couch and took the computer from the coffee table. She put it on her lap and started clicking and typing.

"Are you looking it up?" I said.

She didn't answer.

"Hey, are you looking it up?"

"What?"

"Are you looking it up?"

"What?"

"About Mexico," I said.

"Yeah," she said.

I walked over and looked at the computer screen. It was paragraphs of text with the heading "What You Need to Know About Going to Mexico." I walked into the kitchen and poured water from a pitcher into a glass. I drank it and poured more and walked back into the living room and held the glass out for Carolina to take. She was looking at the computer screen so I put the glass down on the coffee table. "There's water there for you," I said.

"What?" she said.

"Water. There. You," I said pointing.

"Okay, thanks," she said.

It was still morning and we weren't even dressed. Carolina always looked good in the morning.

"You're beautiful," I said looking at her.

"What?" she said.

"Beautiful," I said.

"What's beautiful," she said. "Mexico?"

"And you," I said.

"What?" she said.

"Mexico and you," I said.

"We're beautiful" she said.

"You're beautiful," I said. "Actually, I've only ever been to a border town in Mexico. That time when I went to Arizona, to the south, to ride horses with my friend Anna's family which we never did. We went to a country western bar and sang Johnny Cash karaoke."

"You sang?"

"No, actually, I just watched and drank the Jack and Cokes that kept landing in front of me. Some guy kept calling me Curly."

"That seems weird."

"Yeah. I saw that guy a few days later at some tourist cavern place. I don't think he recognized me, or if he did, he pretended he didn't. He was there with some woman, maybe his wife."

"When did you go to Mexico?" Carolina said.

"The next day, I think, or the day after. We drove down, it wasn't far, crossed the border on foot and walked around the town. It was funny. The Mexican shop owners offered free shots of tequila just to get you inside the stores. The tequila was good too. One guy even said to me, 'Hey, I remember you from high school.'"

"No, he didn't."

"Yeah, he said that. They will say anything to get you in the shop."

"Did you sleep with her?"

"Who, Anna? No. I mean, we slept in the same bed actually but it was a big bed and we didn't have sex."

"Why not?"

"I don't know," I said.

Later that night, I was staring out the window from the bed and I could see the moon was a tiny sliver and very near it was a bright star just off of the inside part of the crescent. I thought about going to Mexico and how nice the sun would be there. I thought about Mexican food and the women with dark black hair. I wondered what one might look like naked, how her thighs would look in a thin summer dress with the sun low in the sky. I looked out the window again and saw the moon there and the star and I thought about how it looked exactly like some country's flag. I couldn't think of which one.

I always thought that Carolina's face was interesting and beautiful, rather than just beautiful, and that she had a certain kind of perfect hair, long and straight the way it was in pictures of her when she was nineteen. She cut the bangs herself and brought them down into her face the same way now as she did back then. She made herself look like old pictures of herself and I think she wanted to be one of them—not her old self, but an old picture of herself. She acted like that sometimes.

I was buying produce at an outdoor farmer's market, thinking about her and the picture thing. It was the end of January by now, but sunny and warm with a light cool breeze. I knew it wasn't going to stay that way for long, so when I got home, before putting the groceries away, I said, "It's gorgeous outside, a good day to be happy, let's get the bikes and go downtown and be happy in the sun."

"A good day to be happy," Carolina said. The way she said it, I knew exactly what to expect. I went into the bedroom to change my clothes, to put my jeans on. She came in and lay on her back on the bed.

"You don't want to go?" I said.

"I don't know. Yoga isn't until two. What time is it?"

"Eleven-thirty," I said.

"What will we do?"

"We'll bike around. We'll go down along the river and bike and be in the sun and it will feel nice and we'll do whatever."

"I don't know," she said.

"It's so nice and it's a good part of the day to be out. It won't last that long. At two you'll be in yoga and by the time you get out the sun will be low and the buildings will be blocking it and the light will go away not long after that and not long after that we'll be back here and then I'll make dinner and we'll eat it and then after that we'll be in bed and the day will be over."

"And then not long after that we will be old and then not long after that we will be dead," she said. I didn't say anything. I looked at her lying there on the bed feeling desperate, looking like she was feeling desperate.

"So you don't want to go?" I said.

"I don't know, maybe just leave me alone a while," she said. I stood there as she got up and walked away from me, out of the room.

"Okay," I said after she was gone.

I heard her in the bathroom and then when she came out she asked where the cleaning stuff was. I didn't know. I didn't say anything. I started looking around in the closets and then I found it. I said, "Here," and handed her some squirt bottles and a sponge.

"You should vacuum," she said taking the things from me.

"Okay," I said. I vacuumed the apartment. I vacuumed it room by room, rugs, hard floors, everything. I moved chairs and sofas, tables, books, beds until I got everything clean. Then I rolled up the cord and put the vacuum cleaner away and sat down and stared out the window at the sunshine and followed it with my eyes into the room and onto my arm.

Carolina came in and sat down in a rocking chair. Neither of us said anything for a while. I could tell she was thinking, and from her face I could see that something was going to happen soon and that it was not going to be pleasant. I sat there waiting, knowing there was nothing to do about it, but that at least I'd be ready.

"I've wasted my whole life," she said.

"No you haven't," I said.

"Yes I have," she said. "I've never finished anything I've started. I'm an eternal student, an eternal beginner at everything. All of that stuff I started doing and then stopped doing to start something else, that stays with me. And it gets worse and worse every year. And I am getting older and losing energy and getting weaker. What is getting better? My mind is getting duller, my body worse. I used to be more beautiful."

"You're beautiful. You and Mexico," I said. Then I said, "I'm sorry that you're going to die someday. You're going to have to let that go at some point or it will be there forever until you do die and maybe longer."

"It's not that I'm going to die, it's that I'm going to get old and be decrepit and useless and everything will still be meaningless and then I'll die," she said.

I didn't say anything. Carolina rocked back and forth in the chair and I looked out the window at the streetlamp and the rust going down its neck. I could see the rust almost straight on from the chair I was in.

"I don't think we have a good energy together," she said.

"You always say that. That is like your fallback sentence when you're feeling terrible about yourself or the world," I said.

"But it's true," she said.

"I don't think it's true," I said, "but maybe you're right. What do I know?"

"And that's a stupid thing to say, 'you have to let it go,' that doesn't mean anything. It's just stupid," she said.

"I know," I said, "you're right. It's stupid. It's stupid."

"I feel like I can't go anywhere or do anything or see anything or anyone because then it is with me forever, haunting me," she said.

"I know." I was looking out the window past the buildings out to the sky.

"I just have to give up and go somewhere where there is nothing. I need nothingness. I need nothingness. I need nothing around me. I need to become a Zen monk, I guess," she said.

I didn't say anything. I looked at her and then out the window again.

"I understand how you feel," I said.

"I don't even know what I'm saying. I don't know what I said," she said.

I didn't say anything.

She said, "What do you understand?"

"What?" I said.

"Tell me what you understand about what I said. I want to know."

"I don't know," I said.

"I want to know what I said, just tell me what I said. I feel like I'm going crazy," she said.

"You said things about how you feel," I said, and then, suddenly, I couldn't remember anything she'd said. I didn't know what she wanted me to say. Instantly she became hysterical—pulling her hair, hitting herself on the head.

"What else?" she said. "What else did I say? I want to know. You said you understood, what do you understand? What did I even say? I feel like I'm getting crazy, really crazy, like for real this time."

"Um," I said, "the thing … things … about … oh, you said, like, the thing about being a Buddhist."

"What?" she said.

"Um …" My voice was low but I wanted to give her real answers. I wanted to calm her down.

"What did I say? I'm so insane."

"You said that we don't have a good energy together and that you need nothingness and to become a Zen monk."

She looked at the floor and didn't say anything. I changed my position in the chair, sliding my leg underneath myself so that I could be higher up and see farther down the hill. I saw across to the tall trees, through some buildings. Carolina got out of the rocking chair and walked past the kitchen into the bathroom. I heard the door shut and later the toilet flush. She came out and went into the bedroom and then from there into the room I was in. She said, "Do you want to take the bikes and go?"

"Yeah, okay," I said.

"Do you want to do yoga today? You can try one lesson for free."

"I don't know," I said.

"Okay, it's fine, I know you don't want to do it, so don't do what you don't want to do," she said.

"No, I want to, I just—okay, yeah, I'll do it." I said.

We took the bikes down the hill going slowly and then we crossed a busy street to get to the river and went along the bike path straight south from where we were. It took twenty minutes to get downtown that way. We rode down along the river away from traffic and it was quiet and the sun was there and the breeze. "If I could always ride my bike in the sun with a cool breeze and do nothing else ever, then that would be okay with me," I said. She didn't say anything. I looked at the side of her face, then the sky.

Eventually we got to where there were cars and people everywhere, and the bike track had ended, so we walked with our bikes through the smaller streets. We locked them to a signpost outside of the yoga center and tried to go inside but the door was locked. "It's weird that the door would be locked. Let me check the schedule," Carolina said. Another woman arrived and Carolina talked to her about the door being locked. The woman rang the doorbell. No one answered and then she rang it again and then someone answered and unlocked the door from inside by pressing a button. The door made a buzzing sound and then I pushed it open.

After yoga, walking with the bicycles to get ice cream, I thought about having been lying there at the end, body very still, looking up at the painted birds on the ceiling. I thought about the blank white walls, I thought about Zen and about monks and about how Thomas Merton accidentally electrocuted himself in Thailand in 1969. I thought about Leonard Cohen bald on the mountain in robes in the nineties. I thought about the line of poetry he wrote which says, "The only thing I don't need is a comb." I thought about everything I had been thinking about as I was lying there with my eyes supposedly shut but looking out just barely through my eyelashes.

Later that night, or the next morning during breakfast, or right before Carolina left the house to have lunch with her ex-boyfriend, she told me I had looked good while doing yoga.

"With your legs all stretched out and your body going in different directions," she said. She was putting some strands of my hair up into braids, an idea she'd had all of a sudden just a few minutes before.

I went into the bathroom to look at myself in the mirror. I said, "These braids are great, why didn't we have this idea before?"

"I don't know," she said.

"We probably did," I said, "we just didn't do it." Then, "You are nice, too, doing yoga. It's so weird, yoga class. It's like dancing."

"No it isn't," she said.

"I know but it's weird," I said, "everyone is there putting their bodies into strange positions that you aren't used to seeing people's bodies in."

She didn't say anything. She was drinking orange juice.

"I just kept picturing people naked. Or, not picturing them naked but just thinking about them naked, or not even that. I was just looking at people and thinking the word naked."

"You are a madman," she said. I laughed and left the kitchen to look out the window. I stood very near to it and looked down onto the street through the leaves at the sidewalk.

Carolina left for lunch and I was in the apartment by myself. It was sunny and warm near the glass. I played Leonard Cohen cassettes that came out distorted. I didn't mind the slower tempos and deeper voice. Sometimes I sat in a chair and sometimes I stood by the window looking out, up and down. There were planes and people and dogs sometimes and sometimes just the evidence of them.

I thought about going to Mexico. I thought about what Mexico would feel like. I touched the braids in my hair, felt them with my fingers. They were pleasant to touch.

Then the sun was covered up by a cloud and the light turned cold white from warm yellow, and then it was back again. I thought about going outside but felt fine just being there by the window looking out, thinking about going there but not going there.

The whole world was still and quiet for a long time as I looked out the window. I heard some birds make sounds in the distance in the trees down by the river and then a crow flew up and landed right on top of the streetlamp. It hopped around for a few seconds and then dove off, right off, down into nothing as if it had been shot or went limp falling motionless. Then I saw it in a tree up the street.

I liked to look at things for a long time without moving when I was by myself. I liked to see how mostly nothing changed much, and when it did it was for a short while and then everything was the same again. After a long enough time of being somewhere, you forgot about all of the little events and interruptions and it was only you that existed with some green leaves and maybe a streetlamp or two, all seen through decorative bars on the window which were there because your balcony was only one story above the street level—something that made it easy to convince your girlfriend to stand on it with you if it wasn't raining outside.

I tried only once to get Carolina to be there with me, very still at the window for a long time, watching how things moved and swayed like looking at an image coming in and out of focus on a screen bordered with window trim.

"So what's this game?" she'd said.

"The game of life," I'd said, "do you know how to play?"

"No," she'd said and left me standing at the window just as it had started to rain hard enough to be interesting to look at. The picture looked different in the rain. Fewer things moved in and out of it, distorting it in one specific spot or another. It wasn't still, moving constantly but slightly, and if you stay there long enough it slows down, becomes normal. And then the next day, when it's sunny, there are colors and angles and the light can seem strange but the streetlamp is there. And the leaves are so green.

The next day it rained again. I stood at the window for a long time. The rain was coming straight down and making small splashes on top of the streetlamp. It gathered at the neck where there were bolts on either side. It was the first time I noticed the bolts. It made the streetlamp look like Frankenstein, lonely and cold and trying to find his clumsy way, and for a second I felt bad for the streetlamp, that it was stuck there in the cement and couldn't move, rusting away. For the first time I thought about it looking at me through the decorative bars on the window, and I saw that it was wearing a top hat with a sleek black ribbon just above the rim, following it around from front to back. Then I realized that I'd never seen the back—that I'd never thought about it—so I went down to the street with an umbrella.

There was no one around. It had been raining a long time and somehow it felt like no one had been around for years. I walked around from the gate of the apartment building to below the window and then crossed the street and stood on the grass plot in front of the building there on the other side. I stood back a few steps and looked up. I thought about how we made a trapezoid from feet to head to head to feet to feet. I wanted to stay there for a long time very still and quiet but it was different being there, out there, a part of it. It wasn't like looking at the picture. There wasn't the frame, and all of a sudden, the decorative window bars weren't between us. I looked up to see the window and there was the body of the streetlamp between it and me.

It was cold outside and the rain made noise on my umbrella. I looked around and there was no one there so I touched the streetlamp and thought about a story I'd read on the news, how a girl got electrocuted from leaning up against a streetlamp in the rain. I thought about Thomas Merton having been electrocuted getting out of the bathtub.

I said, "See you later alligator," and went back inside.

When the sky got dark the streetlamp went on so that I could see the rain passing by in its light. I sat in a chair in the room with the lights on. The lights reflected off the window so that when I looked out I saw the streetlamp and the light from it and the rain going by it, but I also saw the reflections of the lights we had on inside. Carolina was home and sitting on the couch which was between me and the window. She was reading a performance art book and sometimes we talked about performance art ideas. She had made apple crumble that we had eaten, and we drank tea.

I looked out the window at the streetlamp and then moved my eyes down to look at Carolina. She was looking at me. She said, "Yes?"

"What?" I said.

"You were looking at me," she said.

"No, I was looking out the window. Then I looked at you. You must have thought that I was looking at you because my head was turned in your direction."

"Okay," she said.

"Besides," I said, "when I looked at you, your eyes were already looking at me, so you should have seen that my eyes were looking up and not at you, right?"

"Okay," she said.

"Right?" I said.

"Okay," she said.

She looked back down at her book the way she was looking at it before. I looked at mine and saw the pages and the words but didn't read them. I tried to read the words but kept looking out the window over Carolina's shoulder at the streetlamp. I didn't look at her and then I did but she wasn't looking at me. I looked at the streetlamp.

I took a walk down the street and bought a soda and sat on the curb drinking it. It was nice and quiet out. I thought about how anger worked, about all the things you see, hear, smell, touch, about how there's too much in and not enough out. About how that energy has to go somewhere, become something, and how it doesn't help having to be correct all the time, saying the right things at the right times to the right people, all that pressure to be good, never saying too much, never meaning too much with what you say, always appearing cool, calm, collected.

I walked along the streets slow and aimlessly, mostly looking down at the sidewalk, my shoes moving, legs moving, watching stuff move by me as I moved by it. I went back out to a busy street with more noise and activity.

I looked at the branches of a tree, followed them to the long elliptical leaves that were green and moving only slightly. The branches moved most, sometimes just a little and other times more violently, but it didn't seem violent. There is a rhythm to things.

It looked like it might start raining, so I walked back to the apartment under the awnings of all the shops or against the edges of the buildings if there weren't any shops and if there weren't any buildings I tried to stay under the trees.

When I got inside Carolina said, "I've been reading about this man up north."

"Yeah?" I said.

"He calls himself Astroman," she said.

"Interesting," I said.

Astroman lived in Australia and Japan for ten years, studying and practicing permaculture and Japanese natural farming. I think astronomy was just a hobby of his. Carolina wrote Astroman an email about our interest in sustenance farming and eventually buying some land somewhere someday. Astroman wrote back saying that he had lived and worked with 'Masanobu Sensei' for four years—the longest a westerner had ever been allowed to stay—learning about a sort of experimental farming. Popular agriculture would refer to it as experimental, but it was more intuitive and less involved than mainstream farming.

"Do you want to visit him?" she said.

"Sure," I said, "okay."

"When should we go? Should we go with the car?"

"I don't know," I said.

She looked at me and I knew right away, even before she looked at me, that I shouldn't have said I didn't know and that I should have at least said it a different way.

"You don't know," she said, "you always don't know. That is *your* fallback thing to say. You never know. When will you know something or decide something or just care about something?"

I wanted to say I don't know but I didn't. I said, "Are you upset with me?"

"Yes, kind of," she said.

"Why?" I said.

"Because I am tired of being the decision maker. Why does all the weight have to fall on me. You are like some weight that I have to carry around. No, you are like a ghost. You don't even really exist. Who are you? What are you?"

I looked at the streetlamp, then back at her and then back at the streetlamp again. I could tell she was going to ask me why I was looking out the window. I saw it on her face in that second I'd looked at her.

"What are you always looking at out the window?" she said.

"The streetlamp," I said.

"What?"

"The streetlamp."

I made a movement with my head, pointing at it. She turned around and then turned back around and looked at me.

"It's wearing a hat," I said. "A top hat."

She was staring at me. I didn't know why I was saying what I was saying. I hadn't thought it out ahead of time. I felt like I didn't know who was making up the sentences, who was putting the words together.

"Look, it has a hat, and there's a ribbon that goes around. See the ribbon?" I pointed. Carolina looked at my finger going around and then out the window. I looked down at my hand and wondered what would happen next. Everything was happening in slow motion, almost.

"Yes, okay, that does look like a top hat," she said. She was smiling a little. She stopped smiling and was silent for a moment. I stayed standing there, looking at her. I wondered what else was in my head, if anything would come out, what it would be, how it would sound.

"Arthur," she said. She was calm.

"Yeah?"

"Do you think we should split up?"

"You want to split up?"

"No, I don't know. What future do we have? We have no future."

I didn't know what was coming out of her mouth now. She kept her eyes low, her head pointed down at her lap sitting on the couch. She didn't look at me at all. And now there was nothing coming out of my mouth. I opened it and then closed it, realizing I was going to have to think of something to say, on purpose this time, that it wasn't going to happen on its own. It made me feel tired and like collapsing just standing there, to the floor, hitting my head maybe on something. I thought about faking an injury, pretending to be sick, trying to get some pity, trying to get out of the conversation. And then suddenly I had the urge to go to the bathroom and look at my face in the mirror. I wanted to see what my face looked like. I tried to imagine it. I started talking.

"I don't want to split up. I don't know what to do, though, and I'm sorry about that. I am, but I just don't know."

"Why am I always the one trying to figure out our lives?" she said.

"You aren't," I said. "You aren't the only one, I just don't talk about it."

"Well why am I the only one who talks about it, then?"

"Because it matters more to you," I said.

"What do you mean?"

"It matters more to you what happens. You want things to happen."

"Well, why aren't they happening? What are they waiting for? What are we waiting for?"

"I don't know. Something. We are waiting until we want something, or until we do something. We'll do something when we do something, I guess. I don't know what I'm even saying," I said. I thought about how I must not have been making any sense, how I must have sounded like a person who didn't make any sense, like some kind of babbling madman. I wished I was a real madman, safe in a half-way house somewhere, deemed unable to function regularly in society, unfit for responsibility—maybe it was the truth after all.

The conversation went on for a while with Carolina doing most of the talking. I knew why she was frustrated. She had every right to be. I didn't know how I could change, how I could start knowing things, or caring that I didn't know.

Towards the end there was silence for a while in the room. I was standing. Carolina was sitting with her legs up on the coffee table looking out into the air in front of her.

"Can you just go take a walk for a while?" she said.

"I was just out," I looked out the window. "It's raining."

She stretched out on the couch and put a pillow over her face. "Just go into another room then," she said.

I stared at her for a few moments silently, then walked halfway out of the room, the long way, towards the kitchen and stopped, looking at her. She took the pillow off her face and sat up. She looked at me. We were looking silently at each other for a few seconds. "What?" she said.

I shook my head. "I don't—" I said, stopping, and then walked out of the room.

In the back bedroom I stood at the window, looking out, then sat down in an old green armchair and put my feet up. There were a lot of boxes in the room. Not full of anything, empty, waiting to be filled with stuff, the stuff on the shelves and in the closets. Books, clothes, knickknacks, there were lots of knickknacks, and sunglasses, too many sunglasses.

I thought about Carolina, what she was doing there in the other room, what she was thinking about, what was going through her head. I wondered how many more times this would happen in my life, how many more of these we'd go through. I thought about how I never knew what to say. Carolina said what she felt, even if it made her look bad, but she didn't ask to feel those ways, she felt them and she said so. That's what it means to be an honest person. It's not that she tells the truth, it's that living with her is living an honest life, talking with her is having an honest conversation. It's real.

It's what stuff is like. It's what the world is like. There were a lot of ways I felt which I didn't talk about, and sitting there in that room I decided that was the difference. I decided that's what made me angry at nothing in particular, what made me imagine myself slapping a police officer on the sidewalk or pulling the door handle at seventy-five miles an hour somewhere out on the highway. I decided that's what could make me shoot a bunch of people for no reason.

I went quietly out to the kitchen not knowing where Carolina was, and not wanting to find her, but she was there eating a banana.

"Do you want to have lunch?" I said after not saying anything for what seemed like a long time but was probably only a few seconds, eight or nine at most.

"It's late," she said.

"I'll make a salad," I said. She shrugged her shoulders. "Will you eat some if I make a salad?" She nodded her head just one time. I started putting together some lettuce, carrots, and walnuts with a cut up apple. We ate it with olive oil and balsamic vinegar. Carolina sat down at the table and turned on the television while I was making the salad. When I came into the room with the plates and forks, I looked at the television and saw people camping out in the jungle somewhere. I went back into the kitchen, brought out the salad and then sat down at the table. Carolina started putting salad onto her plate.

"Do you want to be in the jungle?" she said.

"Where are they?" I said.

"Africa, I think. There are orangutans. They don't exist in South America, do they?"

"Maybe not."

On the television they were using a stick to clear the ground beneath a hammock that they'd strung up between trees to sleep in. I looked at Carolina. She was chewing.

"Snakes and scorpions won't cross uncovered ground," I said. "They'll go around."

Carolina nodded.

After we'd finished eating Carolina made jasmine white tea in the kitchen. I put cookies on a plate. We stood in the kitchen waiting for the tea to brew. We were standing far away from each other and were looking at each other and then slowly we moved closer. Then we were face to face and I didn't know what was going to be said, what I'd say.

"I was awful," she said.

It felt awkward when we started to hug and then my face got past her face and my head was off to the side of her head and I stared at the wall. We took the tea and cookies into the other room and sat at the table. I was wearing a pale yellow shirt that had an outline of the state of Montana printed on it and the outline of a buck and below that it said: Traditional Bow Hunters of Montana. Carolina was looking at the shirt. She said, "Why does it have the border so straight on the right?"

"What?" I said. We were talking about nothing. It was to make this part of things go by a little easier and faster.

"Montana, the border," she said.

"Oh, because that's the badlands over there. It's just long flat nothingness so I guess they had to draw a border somewhere. They just picked anywhere."

"It's just nothing out there? Not even trees?"

"There are trees in some parts, I think, but there's mostly nothing. Just dusty road. There's not even a speed limit," I said, looking down at my shirt.

"When are we going to start living our life?" she asked.

I said nothing for a while. "We are. Living it," I said. I was impressed with my own restraint, with my choice of words. I said, "It will change, things will happen, stuff will," and all of a sudden I didn't know what I was saying again. I thought what I'd said sounded really dumb. I said it over and over in my head and it sounded dumber every time. I wished I really was dumb so that I couldn't say anything at all. We sat silently for a while and I thought about being dumb, what it would be like.

Carolina said she felt hot, walked to the window, opened it, and then sat down on the couch, picking up a book. I went to the bathroom and then back out to the living room. In the bathroom I looked at myself in the mirror. I thought about my face. I looked at it very closely. I closed my eyes and tried to remember how my face felt before. I concentrated on the feeling, trying to get it back, to get my face back in that expression so I could look at it, but when I did I wasn't convinced that it was the same face.

I left the bathroom and went out to sit in an armchair in the living room. It had green leafy print and was covered with large red and pink flower designs. As I was sitting down, I looked at the chair flowers and then turned my head out towards Carolina and then past her out the window to real flowers.

"It's pouring out," I said.

"Really?" she said.

"Yeah," I said. She was looking at her computer screen now, sitting on the couch with her back to the window.

I could tell that things were turning lighter inside even though the rain was coming down hard out there and at an angle. Not sideways but almost sideways. It was getting dark outside and I saw the rain in a wide beam of orange light, strongest closer to the lamp and weaker furthest away. The tree branches were moving a lot in the wind. We had music on the stereo.

"This album is so good," I said, looking at Carolina. "Can I get an 'amen'?"

"What?"

"I said can I get an amen."

"What are you talking about?"

"You know, I say something true and then say 'can I get an amen' and anyone who agrees with me says it."

She didn't say anything. She was only half paying attention. I was only half paying attention too. The other half of me thinking about what I'd do if we split up, where I'd go. I thought about it with excitement, as though I almost wanted it to happen, and maybe I did.

"This album is so good, can I get an 'amen'?" I said. "Can I get an 'amen'?" I said again.

"What?" she said.

"I said this album is so good, can I get an 'amen'?"

There was a moment of silence and then she said, "Amen."

"Ya gotsa say it wit conviction," I said, emphasizing the word *conviction*.

She looked at me and smiled and said, "Okay, try it again."

"No, I'm tired now." I said, but I wanted it to go on.

"Come on, one more time."

"Can I get an 'amen'?" I said sitting up in my chair.

"No, the whole thing," she said.

"This album is so good, can I get an 'amen'?"

"Amen," she said drawing out the "a." We were quiet for a long time after that. The rain was lighter out the window, more of a mist and not moving at an angle anymore.

"What time is it?" I said.

Carolina didn't say anything. I didn't want to be talking but I didn't want to not be talking. It felt like there was something to say, like if we talked enough about nothing that we would somehow get around to talking about an okay thing.

"It's raining all the time," I said.

"Amen," she said. I smiled and we made eye contact for a few seconds. Then Carolina spoke again. "I just registered on findacrew.net," she said.

"Is that what it sounds like?"

"Yeah, it's great. I made a profile and everything. You should make one too then we can be a team."

I thought about being on a boat together and being in a fight. I wondered who would have to walk the plank. I laughed silently at myself saying *argh matey* in my head. "Do it," I said out loud.

"No, you have to make your own," she said.

"Yeah, you can do it. You know all the information. You have the computer right there. You're online."

"It kind of takes a while. I'm tired of it now."

"Okay," I said, "I'll do it later."

"There's this guy who's going to Malta and some other places, he wants a crew."

"Malta is in the Mediterranean," I said.

"Yeah, I know," she said.

"Where else is he going?"

"I don't know."

"Where is he leaving from?"

"From Sicily to Malta but first he's going across. His boat is located in the Caribbean right now, off St. John, I think."

"Across the Atlantic? That is serious. I really want to do that. Why is he going to Malta? For something specific?"

"I don't know, he doesn't say," she said.

"If we do a cross-Atlantic voyage we get to have tattoo anchors on our forearms," I said.

"I'll read the specs of his thing. Fifty-footer, sleeps seven down in the cabin. Expects crew to pay for all food and supplies for themselves, nothing else. 'I can teach you how to sail,' he says. Earliest sail date is March 10. Latest sail date is March 23. Prefers a wom—oh, it says he prefers a woman aged twenty to sixty."

"What?"

"Do you think he just wants a woman to sleep with?" Carolina said.

"I don't know," I said. "I doubt it."

"Wouldn't it be great to go to Europe by sailboat."

"Amen," I said. Then, "It would be a little scary too. We might run into the perfect storm."

"You saw that movie?"

"On television. I was bored. It sucked but I watched the whole thing. Everyone dies."

"In the whole movie?"

"No, everyone on the boat. It was a fishing boat. They had caught a lot of fish and were coming back home. Oh, whatever, it's stupid, who cares."

Carolina was typing and I was looking at the pages of my book but thinking about being on a boat out on the Atlantic with only blue-gray water and blue-gray sky to look at. I wondered what I'd say to the captain, if I'd even call him captain, what we'd talk about. I was always worried about what I would say to people that I might have to meet, and I didn't like talking to new people while Carolina was around, and she didn't like it either.

"What do you want to do for dinner later?" Carolina said.

"I don't know. Fish?" I said.

She laughed. "You don't eat fish. We don't eat fish," she said.

"Yeah, I know, I was just daydreaming about being out in the middle of the Atlantic. If we did that trip, we'd probably have to eat fish. You can't really be a vegetarian on a cross-Atlantic voyage."

"Yeah, I mean, you could sprout some stuff, but you could never eat enough without eating fish. It's okay though. If we were catching them ourselves, it wouldn't be too bad."

"Yeah, or maybe it would be even worse." I said.

"Yeah, I wouldn't want to have to clean and gut them," she said.

"Yeah."

"So, dinner?"

"I don't know. Feel like going out? Someone should invite us somewhere. Do we know anyone who wants to invite us out to dinner and then pay for it?"

"Probably not."

"I didn't think so," I said.

I realized that the music had stopped. I got out of my seat and put the book down and walked a short distance into the dining room to put more music on. When I went back into the living room I passed my chair to look at Carolina's computer screen. She was viewing other sailboat profiles. I looked out the window. It was dark out, as dark as it would get. The rain had stopped.

A week or two went by pretty quietly. Then came a day when all day long I fell asleep everywhere. Even just after waking, my eyes wanted to be shut. Carolina and I had gotten into an argument the night before about maybe moving out of her Grandmother's apartment and into a new apartment where my dad would have to cosign for us. I made the mistake of saying I had reservations about asking my dad to sign on for something like that when she was always wondering if we should split up. She could see my reluctance when she asked if my dad would be willing to do it. "Oh, he'd do it," I'd said. "He would definitely do it."

"But what?" she'd said.

"But I don't know," I said.

She was mad at me for suggesting that she would stick it to my father somehow if we ended up splitting. I told her that I knew she wouldn't do something like that and that I was only reacting a bit emotionally to her having said it again the other day. I told her that that was my real issue—that she always resorts to that question whenever she's frustrated or confused. We didn't talk it out at the time because that night we'd had a friend over who drank a little too much and stayed until morning. Lying in bed at night, knowing that we'd have to argue in the morning, we were physically as far away from each other as possible. Our bed was two mattresses pushed together on the floor, so we could get pretty far apart. Carolina had whispered that she wanted a divorce. It sounded romantic. I laughed and she said it wasn't funny. "We aren't married," I said.

"Well, I want to get married so that I can divorce you," she said.

"I can see that you are angry," I said.

"Oh, you can? You can you see that?"

"Let's do this in the morning," I said.

"Fine," she said.

We talked things around in the morning, moving words and feelings from one place to another but not getting anything through. It was okay, but I kept my distance the rest of the day. I was careful not to touch her and if I did, I'd apologize for it. She was doing the same.

When we first got together, before we lived together, I remember going to the grocery store to get food for dinner. It was nice walking around together, learning things about each other from how we shopped. At some point then, when we were carrying the stuff in bags out to the car, I said, "It's nice shopping together. It kind of feels like we live together."

"I was thinking the same thing," she'd said, and we'd smiled and then I drove us home and we drank wine and made dinner and love and then love again in the morning. But now that we did live together, grocery shopping was one of the things I hated. We always went to an expensive organic grocery store and walked around arguing about the price of everything and whether or not we needed certain things. Carolina would try to sneak stuff in the shopping cart by putting it under other things while I wasn't looking, but it never worked because I was the one to bag everything at the end so I would see the stuff that was hidden. I guess that was the point though, that by that time it would be too late, and it was, and none of it mattered anyway.

I was still falling asleep all the time. I just wanted to be asleep. I didn't want to be awake. I didn't want to be moving my arms or legs or eyeballs. I just wanted to let their lids shut and be done with it all for a while or maybe forever. I thought about not minding if I never opened them again.

In the morning, a few days later, I sat in the chair parallel to the window and looked out. Looking down from the sky I saw the leaves on the trees and the long thin branches and the streetlamp. I thought about my relationship with Carolina and I wondered what other people's relationships were like. Carolina came out from the bathroom and into the living room. She wasn't dressed from her waist down.

"What should I wear? Is it raining?"

"I don't know, and no."

"Oh," she said.

"Are we going somewhere?"

"I have to go to the bank and put the money somewhere. In something safe."

"Okay."

"Do you want to come with me?"

"What bank are you going to?"

"You mean what branch? I have to go downtown to the main office. Want to go downtown?"

"Alright, yes," I said.

We started walking to the car and then decided to take the bikes, so we biked downtown along the river to where we usually lock our bikes up and then we locked them there. We walked the rest of the way downtown. While Carolina was in the bank I walked around in the streets. I didn't wander far, just down the street and back so I could always see the door, see if she was coming out. I did that about a hundred times. She ended up taking over an hour. At one point, down at the bottom of the street, I thought about drinking a soda. I didn't want to have it in my hand if she came out, though, because I didn't want to have to explain why I wanted one and then bought it and then was drinking it. So I didn't buy it even though I passed the store so many times. After a while I sat on a bench and watched people walk by. A delivery truck came and stopped in just about the only spot that would block my view of the bank's door, but I didn't notice because I had my eyes shut tight. I was playing a little game where I look towards the sun and move around the colors and patterns of light based on how much strength I use when pushing down my eyelids.

When I opened them again it took a few minutes to reset my vision back to normal and then I saw the truck. I didn't know how long it had been there and I thought maybe Carolina had come out so I hurried over to the bank window and looked inside with my hand up against the glass to shade the glare. Carolina was sitting at a desk talking to a bank guy who looked back at me. He waved and she turned around to look and waved too. She turned back around in her chair and they continued talking and looking down and the guy helping her was pointing at pieces of paper on his desk and, I guess, explaining things written on them. I went away from the window and sat on the sidewalk nearby with my back against the wall. After a few minutes, I got up and walked to the next block over and bought a soda and a hot dog from one of the street vendors. I put mustard and ketchup on the hot dog and ate it fast, then I chugged the soda and tossed the empty can into the garbage while walking back towards the bank. I stopped in a convenience store and bought a pack of mint gum and chewed a piece so Carolina wouldn't smell the hot dog on my breath. I went back and sat down on the sidewalk by the bank.

When Carolina came out, we walked to get ice cream. I got strawberry and raspberry in a waffle cone with whipped cream on top and Carolina got chocolate and caramel in a paper cup with whipped cream. When we were walking through the streets towards the good ice cream place, the place that used slow food ingredients, I thought about my parents and how they'd recently redone the rooms upstairs in their house. Sometimes we had to stop at intersections where there were traffic lights. Carolina always pushed the walk button repeatedly as a lot of rows of cars were going by making wind. I told her that it probably didn't really do anything and she shrugged. It happened more than once and then more than that and then it happened so much that it became a sort of joke where she would push the button really fast repeatedly and I would say, "It probably doesn't really do anything." We were sort of mechanical.

When we were bored of that I said we should work on our psychic abilities and Carolina agreed but we didn't do anything. We just kept walking. The sidewalk touched our shoes and I walked looking down like I always did and tried to regulate my steps so that my foot was landing in the same areas between the cracks in the sidewalk. Then I made my walking rhythm match Carolina's and then tried to keep them the same. Sometimes I would switch which leg I led with while still trying to keep my feet landing at the same time as hers. Then I got bored of that and started to take really long steps, to take fewer steps but make each one cover a greater distance, but that put too much strain on my knee so I stopped doing it and asked Carolina if we could walk slower. "It's nice out, let's walk slower," I said. We slowed down for a short while but ended up going back to the same speed as before after not too long. "Let's slow down, we keep speeding up," I said.

"This is the speed I walk at," Carolina said.

"Okay," I said.

Later we were at home on different chairs listening to Joni Mitchell on the stereo. Carolina was looking at the computer and singing out loud along with every song. I was looking at a book and singing quietly along sometimes.

"Can we live in the canyon?" she said.

"Sure thing," I said. It was getting dark outside and I saw the streetlamp turning on, warming up. Carolina was still singing out loud with the music.

"Aren't you Canadian though?" she said.

"What?" I said.

"I was talking to Joni," she said.

"Oh," I said. "Tell her I say hi."

The neighbors, whom I never saw all winter, moved out of their apartment and the superintendent brought in a crew to start remodeling. The noise got so loud sometimes, and the vibrations so strong, that we would shut up as many doors as we could. It was an old apartment with doors still hanging in every doorway, so it worked sometimes, but sometimes it didn't and then we would use any reason at all to leave the house.

One morning just after breakfast they knocked on the door. I was in my underwear making coffee. Carolina answered. They said they'd accidentally busted a pipe and that we wouldn't be able to use the kitchen all day. I got dressed while Carolina called her father and then he took us out for lunch. We met downtown at the fountain in the park. Carolina's father drove his motorcycle so he beat us to the meeting point. He had recently come back from a business trip in Canada where it was below zero degrees. We walked to the restaurant that he had chosen. It was a bit windy out, but otherwise sunny, so it was pleasant to be out. In the shade it was harder.

After we ordered, Carolina and her father talked about whatever. I wasn't paying attention. I was thinking about Carolina's father coming into the city down the highway on his motorcycle. I was picturing him passing cars on either side, down the middle, getting through traffic easily. I wondered what he'd thought about. If it was just the directions, the lights and the turns he had to make, or if he thought about how his wife, whom he hadn't lived with for five years, wouldn't give him a divorce the easy way, or if it was something else. I often wondered what it was he thought about inside his head while other stuff was happening. I wondered what he thought of me, about how I didn't have a job or any money or ambition. It didn't seem much like he cared, and he wasn't the type of guy to ever mention those sorts of things, but I wondered what he really thought. He was separated from two wives. First Carolina's mother, a long time ago, when she was young, and more recently from another woman with whom he'd had a son who was now seventeen or eighteen and impregnating girls of his own.

He was a nice enough guy, Carolina's father, funny and easy to be around most of the time. He was a little restless in the life department, particularly with women, but that didn't have anything to do with me. I thought about if Carolina and I split up, what would he think of it. He would probably understand. He'd been through it enough times. I wondered what sort of person wouldn't understand it, wouldn't understand why people sometimes split up even if they want to be together. I thought about how I didn't really understand it myself, but how it was a different kind of non-understanding, one that was accepting.

Carolina's father ordered wine and poured it into our glasses when it arrived. I ate some sesame sticks that came in a little package in the bread basket. He talked about his job and how they were going to promote him soon even though he didn't want the new job.

"I don't even want the one I have now," he said and then laughed. Carolina excused herself to the bathroom.

"What's the new position?" I asked.

"Director of Operations," he said. I knew he worked at a hospital, but he didn't seem to want to talk about it too much, so I didn't push it. When Carolina came back from the bathroom I took my turn. I didn't pee though, I just walked in there and stood looking in the mirror and then I washed my hands. I went back out to the table and they were talking about something else. They were talking about Carolina's father's five-year-old son. He was her half-brother. His name was George. "Not for George Bush, though," his father always said.

Later I asked Carolina what all that about her father's job was and she told me that they were going to promote him to be the director of the hospital. She said he'd been saying for a while that he wanted to go back to being a physician and making house calls to people who couldn't get out for whatever reason. He had done that when he was young and that's what he wanted to go back to.

After lunch we walked around in the streets for a little while. It was February 14 and lots of people were holding hands. There were street photographers going around looking for that sort of thing.

We were on the couch. We had moved a floor lamp from the spare bedroom into the living room right next to the couch because Carolina wanted a light to read by. Sometimes Carolina turned on all the lights in the room and then there was so much glare that I could barely see outside at all.

We went to a park nearby to walk around a dirt track which had dried out pretty well since the last time we were on it, and Carolina's feet kept sinking into the mud. She wore ultra-thin shoes with a separate compartment for each toe so that you can walk around on the ground outside and get it pretty close to being barefoot. The sole is thin black rubber that is supposed to be ultra-durable. They say the word "ultra" a lot when marketing these shoes: ultra-light, ultra-thin, ultra-durable, ultra-protective, ultra-bare—that one I didn't get, how could ultra-bare be anything less than bare? Or anything more than bare, or whatever.

I'd gotten these shoes for her when I went home to visit my parents because I knew she wanted them. Every time she wore them, people would look at her feet and ask about them. She always said, "They're called Five-Fingers." And then I always said, "Which doesn't make sense because they're for toes." Then she pressed the walk button and I said I didn't think it worked that way.

Back at home, we were on the couch again. It was dark now. The floor lamp was on. I just stared at the window.

I noticed that I spent less time looking outside when it wasn't raining. I guess there wasn't as much to know then. Sometimes I would look through the window at the sky for a long time and watch the clouds if there were any. Carolina was always inside on the computer trying to figure out our life. I didn't understand her compulsion but I guess maybe I did. Maybe she thought that things needed to happen soon for her. It didn't matter how many examples I gave her of successful people who didn't become successful until much later in life. Or people we knew who were older than us and in a similar position. She had this need to prove that she was good, that her existence was valuable. I didn't know if it would ever ease up. I wondered if I would feel the same way at some point.

In the morning I made orange juice for Carolina—squeezing it out the manual way—and then brewed coffee for myself and tea for her, then I sat down in a chair and looked out the window. Carolina was on the couch with the computer on her lap.

I put some music on so there'd be something in the air that might keep us from talking about anything so early on in the morning before the sun even had the chance to get up over the buildings. I was imagining the conversation in my head, about what should we do and that we don't know. I wanted to be the streetlamp. I wanted to be the trees or just the branches of the trees, a bird, a frog, something with a different kind of consciousness. I wanted to suggest to Carolina that we ought to try and do more things our separate ways, try and spend more time apart so that it would be nicer when we were together again. I didn't know how to do it, what to say, what to suggest. I didn't know what I'd even do, where I'd go, but I thought I might figure out something. I thought it might be good to be on my own sometimes. I wanted to be. That's why I liked doing the dishes or the laundry or vacuuming, taking out the trash— because I did them on my own and it was just me. When I would take out the trash, if it was a nice day with the sun, I would take it to the farthest dumpster and walk around a few blocks before going back the long way. I often spent those walks wondering what Carolina was doing, how she was feeling, what I would have missed by the time we saw each other again.

Then I went to the coast one morning, a few mornings later, having decided it with Carolina at breakfast. There was the apartment there that had been owned by Carolina's grandmother which had passed on to her father when she died. It was the top floor of a three-story building next to others that were like it, on a part of the ocean where there wasn't a beach. It was all rocks, big ones, with a few stony beaches to the right but you had to take out a cushion if you wanted to lay yourself there and you couldn't really swim because there were huge thorny urchins hidden in the rocks in the water. There were sand beaches ten or fifteen minute's walk up the coast along the rocks, or you could cut across the landscaped lawns if no one was watching and make it in under ten.

I went with a few things in my backpack, took the bus because we didn't know how long I'd stay and Carolina's father needed the car every Saturday with the little child's seat strapped in the back. It was his car and he was her father. I was finally on my own for a while. There was an old bike on the little balcony facing the street that I could use to get around, but walking would be fine too.

Carolina always said she felt much better there on the coast. She had grown up going there in summers and winters—any time of year really if she just wanted to get away from the city for a while. She had lost her virginity there with her boyfriend when she was twenty and he was nineteen. It was somehow easier for Carolina to have sex by the ocean than in the city, that's what she would say. She never felt the right kind of energy from the city. The sun and the sea and the clean air and maybe just the great big presence of the water and the sky above the water. It was calm and it passed into her, more than it did for me, and that relaxed her. Or if it was stormy, it was a good kind of stormy that passed different energy into her and we went with it. Those nights were interesting.

I liked being there on the coast, especially in the winter with it empty and cold, not feeling like a beach town was supposed to feel. But I could feel okay just about anywhere, so I wondered why we were doing it this way and not the other way around, but we were.

❖

The furniture in the apartment had a vacation-y feel to it. They were old seventies-style sofas, a mix of sky and water blue with big red lobsters crawling around imprinted on it. There was a three-cushion sofa and two armchairs that matched, and there was a bench seat on the wall that had two one-piece cushions that met to make a right angle. I put my backpack down on that and opened all the windows. I went out to the street balcony to check out the bike and turn on the gas, open the water, and switch on the water heater. With the windows open there was a strong airflow through the living room and down the hallway. Sometimes it pushed the terrace doors shut and I worried about the glass breaking so I latched them. The window opposite the street side, towards the east, was gigantic and had a view of the ocean. I leaned out of it with my elbows resting on the roof of the balcony that belonged to the apartment below me. That first day, I leaned out that big window about a thousand different times before going away and doing something else and then coming back.

We had been together a long time and being together was complicated now so it was easy to be at the beach apartment by myself. There was a little stereo and I could listen to anything I wanted and cook whenever I wanted to cook, whatever I wanted to eat. If I wanted to have a soda, I went into town and bought one. If I wanted to, I could smoke a cigarette without having to brush my teeth and wash my beard immediately afterward.

I rode the bicycle around town and down along the rocks, in the open field next to our building, even on the bigger road sometimes, and one day I rode for a couple of hours up the coast and then just turned around and rode back. I was tired when I got back and feeling sleepy on the couch in the sun so I let myself sleep. It didn't matter if I wouldn't sleep at night or be hungry for dinner or if I'd be hungry early. It was uncomplicated to exist as only one person with one set of needs and wants, one set of feelings and moods that did what they wanted. It was easy not having to coordinate anything, not having to balance out anything or force in or out anything. It was comforting to know that it was just me with me and that I couldn't leave myself or if I did it wouldn't matter then because I would be crazy for real. In that case someone would come get me and things would be decided for me and that might be better.

I found a bird's nest in a hole in the terracotta roof tiles that covered the little storage section of the big terrace. There were three or four little baby birds chirping all the time except for when I went close by them near the nest and they pulled themselves inside to hide until I went away again, and I did and I let them be safe.

Sometimes it was lonely at night and my mind would get on thinking with all the quiet darkness around. And sometimes lying in bed listening to the moon pull the ocean in and out, I touched myself quietly so that I could fall asleep. I could have made all the noise in the world, could have made a mess, done whatever, but for some reason I was silent and clean.

Walking on the beach sometimes I saw people and they were there and I was there and sometimes we looked at each other and sometimes we didn't. Sometimes when looking at each other we smiled. Sometimes the other person was a girl and if it was then I imagined her naked there walking on the sand in the wind that was a little bit cold and then her body tensed and her thighs got tight as did all the parts of her body that I was imagining. I didn't know how to imagine what some parts looked like all tight and I thought about asking her to come back with me and show me but I never did. I never thought about it seriously as a real option, only as a dreamy one and sometimes I would hurry back to the apartment and think about it in a different way.

One night I slept out on the terrace for no reason at all. I did it because I had the idea to do it, to see the sky and stars, or just to do something I didn't usually do, and nothing got in the way of that. It was a cold night. Partway through the night I went inside and slept on the couch because it was so cold, and I had dragged the mattress and all the sheets outside and I didn't want to bring them back in half-asleep. The couch was uncomfortable and by morning I hadn't slept well and my head felt dense as I made coffee, but drinking it helped. I thought about how Carolina would have stopped me from sleeping outside by saying that it was a stupid idea, and about how I would have been upset and acted childishly by laying myself down on the far side of the mattress and then getting up early in the morning before we usually got up and being in the other room. I thought about how I would have at least slept and would be feeling normal now in the morning instead of how I was feeling, and then about how after a tentative breakfast everything would be okay and we would go out walking in the sun and smell the salt. Somehow that salt in the air could dissolve anything.

I thought about leaving the apartment, about getting on a boat going somewhere, a freighter, or hopping on a freight train headed north or west or south, not telling anyone. I wanted to go and not stop going and never stop going but I knew that at some point I would be stopped somewhere and I wouldn't feel so great and I would think about how I made a mistake just going away like that, and how doing a thing like that changes you into the type of person who does those things, which I wasn't and didn't really want to be. I wanted to not have to make a decision about anything ever again. I wanted to float around in the air and let someone grab my string and pull me along. If no one wanted to, I would just go up and up and up and eventually choke a beautiful harmless bird. I thought about how childish I was, how I was just a child who couldn't take care of himself, who couldn't plan ahead, think for the future, who could only think to fulfill basic momentary needs.

I didn't know how to make it work with Carolina. I didn't know what I could do, how to decide things for more than one person. I thought about how then, there at the beach on the edge of a huge mass of land and a huge mass of water, I wanted to say "I don't know" to whatever anyone asked me for the rest of my life. If someone asked me what I wanted to do, I wanted to say "I don't know" and I wanted to say that I wanted to say "I don't know," and that I'd decided that I was always going to say "I don't know" because I didn't know, I didn't ever know. I didn't know and I didn't care and maybe that was the real reason that I didn't know.

I opened the big ocean-view window and put my face out in the breeze. I thought about what I'd make for dinner as it darkened outside. With the light disappearing I felt calmer and then it got very dark and I didn't turn any lights on. I sat down on the sofa in the darkness and hung my head back, looking at the sky behind the window. Then I got up and walked to the wall to turn the kitchen light on and I made myself something to eat and then I ate it.

After putting the dishes in sink water, I read quietly by a small lamp in the living room and wondered what Carolina was doing, if she had been with anyone or just by herself. I wondered if she'd gotten fed up with it all and gone to bed with an old friend or someone new. I thought about which one would be better, which one I'd care less about and then decided that it didn't matter, that I didn't care, and that I wished she were there with me in the room then, making it smaller.

Later, lying in the darkness not sleeping by the moonlight reflecting off the water, I told myself that everything in the whole world wasn't my fault. I told myself that babies dying in Darfur wasn't my fault, that kids shooting each other in school wasn't my fault, that global warming and peak oil weren't my fault, the trouble in the Middle East wasn't my fault, the financial crisis wasn't my fault. Over-aggressive fish farming, slaughterhouses, GMO, the old man in our building, hunched over, who could barely make it down for the mail and back: all not my fault.

In March sometime, Carolina came out with the car and a new haircut. I thought I'd be ready for her, but things might be awkward at first. We wouldn't get too close. We'd talk about nothing for a while, getting the nothing out before we could get into something else. Then somebody would smile and we'd lean out the window together the same as I'd done before when I'd first arrived and many times by myself after that.

"Isn't it so nice here?" she'd say.

"It is."

"Don't you love me here?"

"I do," I'd say. Then, "I love you everywhere."

"But a little more here."

"Maybe a little more here."

"Yes, more here."

"Maybe a little."

We'd touch for the first time in a small way there by the window, and feel happy that the sun was there with us, and that we were there.

But when I heard the car I went to the window looking out over the little parking lot, and saw her legs in jeans and the wind pushing her shirt against her breasts and then the boyish haircut with some strands at irregular lengths. "You cut your hair," I said.

She looked up at the window and shielded her eyes from the sun. "It's a surprise? Do you like it?"

"Yeah. Yes. It's a good surprise," I said.

After she came up the stairs and into the apartment she said, "Feel the back, it feels good."

"What else can I touch it with?" I said with my hand there gently.

"Very funny," she said.

The energy wasn't awkward at all. The haircut changed it. It felt like we were a fisherman couple away from each other for many months against our will because of work and no other reason, and that I was coming home to my lady, only that my hair had grown long out on the water and was now much longer than hers. I even had the beard for it.

We took a walk on the beach in our bare feet in the sun. The wind was there too but just a little bit. We walked with our bodies close together.

When we went back to the apartment, we made love because it was lunchtime and the market was closed while the owner was home eating. There was no one else in our building, no one at all, all the windows were shut up and the shutters were shut up too. We made love on the couch. We had started it outside but when I got her pants off she was too cold so we went back inside. We sat upright for it and at an angle so Carolina could see out the window to the water, and afterwards when we stayed still for a long while leaning against each other, Carolina kept watching the water as it moved on an angle from the point that jutted out up towards the gentle rocky coast we were on.

We felt like we needed each other a little less and wanted each other a little more, thought about it silently to ourselves without much concentration before getting up and getting cleaned up. Then we went to buy some fresh produce because there was plenty of dry food in the cupboards.

We put the food in the car and walked from where it was parked to the only cafe that was open. It was on the beach access road that ran parallel to the coast, up and down. We sat out back in the sun with the sand and the shells and the water just over a little wooden railing that I rested my elbow on. We took milk with our coffee and I had them put some whiskey in mine instead of milk. Carolina read the international news section of the paper we bought and I read the funnies. I called them the funnies when I was asking Carolina for the section. "Can I see the funnies?" I'd said.

"The funnies?"

"Yeah. The funnies."

"Alright, here you go grandpa, do you need your spectacles?"

I skipped most of the comics because when I came to one with more than twenty words or so, I'd just glance at it and then move on to the crossword or read something stupid in the advice column. I read one or two of those, sitting there in the sun by the ocean. One was about some lady whose son left home when he was sixteen and now is twenty-four and never comes to see his mother since the last time he had come when he'd gotten angry and threw things and broke stuff.

I read the whole thing through and then the back-story of it. It was some kind of on-going communication through the paper between this woman and a tarot therapist. They'd had her get a deck of a certain kind of tarot card and choose three cards and report which ones they were in the paper, but she wasn't allowed to get the cards herself. She had to have someone buy them for her because they'd only work if they were gifted. I guess she managed it, because the next week they'd given her a synopsis that said her son left home and stayed away because he was taking on the archetypal role of the man and that it meant that in their case she must have not wanted the father around at the time the son had been conceived, which apparently was exactly the case, although I don't think they ever told her how to resolve the issue. Maybe that wasn't the point.

"You have to read this thing," I said while tapping the railing lightly with the paper in my hand. Carolina was sitting across from me silently, as she had been for a long time.

"Did you know that you can be arrested for stealing someone's wireless?"

"What?" I said.

"Wireless Internet. Some guy was on a bench outside somewhere in London using an open connection and he got arrested."

"Maybe that can happen in London but I don't think it's happened here."

"Can you believe that can even happen? It's unbelievable, as you would say."

"Unbelievable," I said.

"Yeah, like that, unbelievable."

"Unbelievable," I said again.

"You always say it, and just like that, unbelievable."

"Unbelievable," I said. Then I said, "You have to read this thing, anyway. Some correspondence from a tarot reader and a woman who has a problem with her son," I said. Carolina didn't say anything so I stopped talking about it.

"Where are we going to get Internet, anyway, out here?" I said.

"Why do you keep saying anyway?"

"I don't know."

"There's a police station up the road. They probably have wireless and I bet they don't protect it, being all the way out here in the middle of winter. There might not even be anybody in there and I bet they don't turn it off. We could park on the road nearby and try to get the signal, if we're discreet."

"Or we could go at night."

"Do you think they'd find out?"

"Maybe, but what harm could it be anyway as long as we weren't doing anything bad, like trying to access their servers or whatever. They might just yell at us or just tell us we can't do it," I said.

"Who needs the Internet anyway? We've got the beach up there and all that water and the sky and those rocks. Those rocks are nice. Look how rocky they are."

"Yeah. I see that, charming," I said.

"But the sky, anyway, the sky."

"We have the sky everywhere."

"Not like we have it here. Here it's all ours. There's nobody else even looking at it except maybe out on a ship way on out on the horizon."

"Yeah and that's international waters so it doesn't count," I said.

"Is it really?"

"Yes ma'am. Past three miles off of every shore is international waters, I believe."

"That's not three miles."

"I reckon it that way."

"Why are you talking like that?"

"I don't know, but it is. The human eye can see seven miles to the horizon, and that ship isn't far off the horizon."

"It's not at the horizon. If that ship is seven miles away then it is gigantic, and it's not gigantic so it isn't seven miles away."

"Well even if it's half way there, it's still over three miles so that makes it international waters and that means they don't count," I said.

"Why does being international waters mean they don't count? And if I give that one to you, then what if they are less than halfway to the horizon? I'll give you one but not the other."

"This is getting complicated." I said.

"But what if they're less than three?"

"Well they aren't. They are more than three."

"How do you know?"

"Because I have better vision than you, so there."

"Okay, fine, let's hear it about the other part then."

"What other part?" I said.

"The international waters thing."

"Oh, that, you ask anybody about that, they'll tell you."

"I don't want anyone else to tell me. I want you to tell me."

"I'll tell you and then I'll kill you," I said.

"Oh, then you'd better not tell me. That could get messy."

"Yeah, and if we're going to steal wireless Internet from the police maybe we shouldn't kill anybody, each other or elsewise."

"Elsewise?"

I laughed. "I don't know, whatever. I meant otherwise I guess or else-something, who could know?"

"Maybe those people out in international waters."

"Oh, so they are in international waters now are they?" I said.

"We agreed to that much."

"What were we even talking about?"

"I don't know," she said.

"Good," I said.

We paid and walked back to the car slowly, staying on the side of the street with the sun. We drove the six minutes back to the apartment, parked, and went upstairs.

"I'm going to take a bath," Carolina said when we got inside.

"Alright," I said.

I went into the kitchen and rooted around the cabinets and shelves. I brought out an ageless bottle of rum from the liquor cabinet, looked at the back label, and then put it down on the counter.

I looked at some old history-of-the-town books on a bookshelf, black and white photographs, pre-development stuff. Then I realized we'd forgotten the groceries out in the car so I grabbed the keys from the hook near the door which was screwed into an old piece of driftwood that had been hung on the wall and went down for them. When I came back, I cut up some fruit: one banana, two apples, three kiwis. I found the blender in the cabinet, cleaned it, and put the fruit inside with a little bit of milk and ice. When the texture became smooth and consistent I got out a shot glass and filled it up three times, putting it all in the blender. I mixed it a short while again and then poured it into two cocktails glasses with a little left over.

We drank them sitting out on the terrace which was almost as big as the whole apartment inside. There was a retractable awning near the door that you couldn't bring out on really windy days because it was made of cloth and would blow around too much and you'd never be able to get it back, but the day wasn't too windy so I pulled it out all the way and tied the rope off on a flower pot filled with concrete like tying a ship to the dock. We sat low to the ground in lounge chairs with cushions on them positioned beneath the awning so that our faces were in the shade and the sun was on our bodies. It was getting down low in the sky now so we had to move the chairs every so often to keep our faces out of the sun so that we could see what we were reading or looking at. Before I'd even tried my drink Carolina had finished hers and was waving the glass at me from her chair while looking down at a magazine.

"You're done already? You have to drink slower," I said.

"Is there any more?"

I took the glass from her and went back inside to the kitchen and poured the rest into her glass, then I poured in a little more rum. When I put the glass on the tile floor next to her I said, "Better make it last, this one."

She took a sip of it and said, "Whoa, this is strong."

"Yeah, I guess the rum sank to the bottom," I said. "You don't want it?"

"No, want it, me, want it," she said.

I sat down looking at the waves of the ocean coming in against the rocks and felt a bit sleepy so I rested my head sideways against the chair. The sun was there and a breeze which I saw pushing around Carolina's short soft hair before I closed my eyes. I kept them closed for a long time but didn't sleep. I thought about the sea and the ships, the birds making sounds in the air above the water, and the ones being quiet in the roof not far from where I was sitting. I thought about the food chain, about the fish in the water, the big ones eating the small ones, the people eating the big ones. I thought about the rocks and the waves and the air and everything else that was around and moving or being still. I thought about the lamppost at home outside the apartment window, and about all the other lampposts in the world. I thought about Carolina and me, about how we might be alright if we could live in different places and just see each other sometimes, or how we might be alright the way things were, without changing anything, about how it was nice to think so anyway. I thought about how we needed to be by ourselves and with each other at the same time, about how we couldn't even decide on that, about how we didn't know what to do, how we wouldn't ever know, and how it was nobody's fault.

"Do you think we knew each other in a past life?" Carolina said.

I didn't answer right away. I wasn't thinking about the question, I was thinking about which word felt better to say, which word wanted to come out of my mouth.

"Yeah," I said.

"You do? How?"

"It's just nice to think so, I guess."

"Yeah," she said.

I didn't say anything.

"Whatever it is. I don't know what it is, but it's something," she said.

"Yeah," I said.

"I think I felt that you were feeling it. Were you feeling it just then?"

"I was feeling something," I said.

We were silent for a while. My eyes were still closed. I felt the breeze come past Carolina's hair onto the side of my face. She shifted her position.

"Do you think we're going to make it?" she said.

"We'll figure something out," I said. "But when we do I think we're going to miss it a little."

"Miss it?"

"Needing to figure something out."

Eventually the sun dropped so low it reached all the way across the terrace and I imagined a big sparkling line out on the water that moved as your point of view did. I heard Carolina dragging her chair across the tile, and felt the warm sunrays on my face. I put my head back into the atmosphere. I thought about the particles of nitrogen and oxygen and about how there was some ice moon far off orbiting another planet that might have life frozen intact deep inside some ancient glacial lake.

The End

For who knows what is good for a man in life, during the few and meaningless days he passes through like a shadow? Who can tell him what will happen under the sun after he is gone?

Ecclesiastes 6:12

Matthew Savoca was born in 1982 in Pennsylvania and now lives in New York and Pennsylvania, where he works as a carpenter. His other books include *long love poem with descriptive title* and *Morocco* (which was written with Kendra Grant Malone).

Find out more at www.MatthewSavoca.com.